Wife

Elle

DEDICATION

This book is dedicated to those with self-doubt, the people who are scared to work towards their dreams because of fear of failing or not having the support of others. Take it from me – dream big, apply yourself, love yourself, and push yourself to do more and be more. Anything is possible!

CONTENTS

ACKNOWLEDGMENTS

I want to thank my family and friends for continuing to support me and believing in me, even when I didn't believe in myself. I want to thank my sisters for always pushing me to know that I am a queen and I am loved. Especially, I want to thank my mom for always inspiring me to hustle and get things done on my own. I appreciate you. Lastly, I want to thank my past for making me into the woman I am today.

A Note from the Author

This book is my first of many novellas. Creative writing has been a passion of mine for as long as I can remember, and I'm truly grateful to explore this opportunity to share my art with the world. Thank you, from the bottom of my heart, for your support. I look forward to sharing more works of fiction with you in the near future.

INTRODUCTION

Nearly every little girl dreams of her wedding day.

Cliché, maybe, but it's true.

She dreams of the day when she'll wear a beautiful white gown and long, flowing veil and walk down the aisle to meet the man of her dreams while her guests take out their tissues to wipe away happy tears during the love-filled, sappy ceremony.

As I got older, those dreams grew grander and more detailed. I loved love, and I always knew I'd be an amazing wife. My loyalty and dedication were always unmatched, maybe to a fault, but that was me and I knew no other way to love than to love deeply. When dreaming about my future wedding, I even envisioned my bouquet, an arrangement of blood red roses tied with a thick, ivory-colored ribbon to offset the green stems, and I had a few bridesmaids in mind, too. I always kept to myself, even at a young age, but there were a few women I wanted by my side if and when my big day rolled around.

My big day arrived sooner than I anticipated. I got married when I was 24 years old, but I didn't have the elaborate gown or the long lace veil, and I definitely didn't have the beautiful bouquet of blood red roses, either, but I believed I had the man of my dreams, Camron, by my side.

Well, kind of...

I met Camron five years ago in 2014. Well, we didn't exactly "meet". He slid in my DMs on Twitter, but I mean, we live in a digital world, so I wasn't opposed to getting to know someone from social media. I had a man at the time, but our relationship was on the outs. I've never been one to cheat, so I let Cam's DM sit in my inbox until the relationship with my ex came to an end which happened to be a couple of weeks later. I liked Cam's persistence, though. It turned me on.

Cam continued to DM me, constantly sending me his phone number and asking for my number in return. A man who knows what he wants is a plus, and I had a feeling this was going to be much more than a conversation confined to Twitter DMs. Even though I didn't immediately reply to his message, that didn't stop me from reading through his tweets. From the looks of it, Cam was on the quest to be a famous rapper. His Twitter was full of re-tweets, sound clips, self-promotion, and everything you can imagine from an up and coming musician. His name didn't really ring a bell, but I listened to his sound clips online and he sounded dope. He definitely had talent but had yet to blow up on the rap scene let alone the down South circuit. I guess it was only a matter of being discovered.

Nevertheless, I eventually answered Cam's DM, and our DMs turned to texts which turned to meeting in person, and from the moment we met, we couldn't keep our hands off each other. Our attraction was crazy. From staying up all night and laying up under each other to dates to STK and finger-fucking under the table to making love just about everywhere, our connection was undeniable, almost unhealthy because we were moving so fast. We wanted each other, and we felt as though we needed each other, too. I was his biggest cheerleader, and he was my ultimate supporter, too. This was more than sex. We shared a connection.

Before Cam's rise to fame, he exuded ambition. Granted, up and coming rappers in Atlanta are a dime a dozen, but he was different. He was always a smart, driven man, two of my favorite qualities in a partner. He never complained about putting in the work, even when his return wasn't much to write home about, and yet I admired his consistency. The truth is, I knew I was in love with him from the day we finally met in person. I fell fast, and I fell hard, but I didn't care nor was I scared. It felt right. He felt right. From the moment we met, sparks flew. We shared our dreams, constantly laughed together, and we talked about shit that mattered. He was my homie and my man, something I always wanted in a relationship. Camron was sweet, thoughtful, and patient, a man who left random "thinking of you" notes in my purse and surprising me with small bouquets of flowers. He didn't have much at the time, but he did everything in his power to make me smile. In my heart, he was already a star, even though no one knew who he was, and his music wasn't played by people outside of his immediate circle and a few local clubs. He deserved stardom and wealth, at least I thought he did, but when that day finally arrived, the fame and money went to his head faster than I ever imagined. The man who used to rock fake rings that turned his fingers green became a man I hardly recognized, a thoughtless, cold-hearted man with only his needs and wants in mind, a materialistic man who didn't care who he hurt. The man I met in 2014 was nothing like the ruthless man he is today, and although our journey has been wild as hell, I always seem to wander back to memories of the good times. Isn't that how it always goes? You hold on to what feels familiar and what feels good yet somehow block out the bullshit. Well, that's how it went for me for quite some time. Stupid, I know, but matters of the heart are hardly ever rational.

We both had big dreams, and I loved that we rooted each other on as we moved towards our goals. Our relationship may have started off as physical, but it grew to a place where I truly felt as though I was with my very best friend. My dreams became his dreams, and my goals became his priorities.

"I want to put my thoughts on paper," I would say to him as we laid on my bed. "I want to write a book. I want to be an author, and I want to make this happen. I see myself doing so much with my life," I would share with him, hardly able to contain my excitement about my dreams of being a writer.

"Babe, you can do this!" he always encouraged, totally excited about my dreams and how our futures were bound to take off together. He became more hype than me over my goals, urging me to go for it, make a plan, and live my best life. He may not have understood my passion for writing, but he loved my ambition. Writing wasn't my only goal, though. I also wanted to work in the medical field, and Cam loved the fact that my dreams weren't confined to one specific goal. "You can do anything you put your mind to, and anything I gotta do to help, I got you," he would insist, and he meant it. I felt it. I loved the way he believed in me, and my confidence grew because of the love and faith he put into my dreams. Isn't that what love is about, making each other better and encouraging one another, too? There was no doubt that we were one another's biggest cheerleader, but love is more than rooting each other on and sharing the same level of ambition. If it wasn't, we probably wouldn't have had so many damn problems.

Camron may have had big dreams back then, but he didn't have his own place. In fact, he lived with his grandmother in Alpharetta, Georgia, the country outskirts of Atlanta, not the ideal situation but starving artists usually can't afford a place in the city, not a nice place, anyway. Cam would grab a change of clothes from his grandma's house and come back to my house, every day, but the commute became a hassle. Traffic to and from Atlanta has always been a bitch. Gridlock by way of 285 or any other major road is hell. So, instead of driving back and forth to see me, he wound up staying the night at my place.

I loved every minute we spent, but my sister certainly didn't. At the time, I shared a condo in Midtown with my sister, Brittany, and she couldn't stand Cam's ass. She didn't want him to come over, and she definitely didn't want him to spend every night at our condo. She didn't see the side of Cam I happened to love, but I figured if she gave him a chance, she would begin to like him.

"He ain't shit, Jaz!" she would say. "You can't see through him? I mean, damn, the man is no good!"

Brittany may be my little sister, but our 12-month age difference basically makes us twins. We're as thick as thieves, and when she told me she could smell Cam's bullshit a mile away, I should've listened. Signs were blatant from the start, but I saw potential in this man. Worse, I was dickmatized, and there's nothing worse than a smart woman going gaga over some dick, but hey, that was the truth. Family always knows best, and I should've listened to my sister, but should've, would've, could've, right? Brittany's dislike for Cam was more than her intuition telling her he wasn't shit. Once, she saw Cam getting picked up from our condo by some chick. Then, my best friend at the time knew he was sleeping with some stripper from Lollie's. Naturally, he denied and downplayed both situations. Then, there were the texts I found in his phone, messages here and there that made it seem as though he was a single man on the prowl.

"That's just my little sister," he lied so convincingly when I approached him about the stripper.

"Nah, that's my homegirl. I needed a ride to the studio really quick," he swore when I mentioned the girl who picked him up outside my condo.

"Jaz, that ain't nobody," he would say as he brushed off my questions about his questionable texts to other women.

You know, typical lies niggas tell. I never caught him in the act of cheating, so I couldn't exactly say he followed through with sex with another woman, but it was undeniable that he introduced and entertained the idea. Nevertheless, when my sister spotted him getting in someone else's car, my relationship with Cam was just starting out, so I figured he would eventually calm down with his wild ways. After all, we were newly dating, so I let some shit fly under the radar.

The same year, in 2014, Cam's career started picking up steam and he ended up making enough money to get his own place, a place I eventually moved into. Two months from the day we met, I officially moved into his apartment.

"Pick a hand," he said as he held two fists out in front of me, prompting me to choose a hand for whatever reason. Cam was a jokester, so I figured he was having me play some random little game.

I laughed, played along, and chose his right hand, and he slowly opened it to reveal a key.

"Move in with me, Jaz," he said, smiling from ear to ear as he held up the key to his new place. From that day forward, I moved into his new apartment with him.

Our relationship was like a car without brakes, rushing down the highway at full speed, but the shit felt good. Weirdly, I liked a little bit of chaos in my life. I've always been a planner and super stable, and I always had my shit together, but with Cam, life was slightly unpredictable, and I can't even lie but I loved it.

I may have been blinded as fuck by love and lust, but one thing was for sure – he had a good woman in his life, and that wasn't up for debate. If only he had matched my energy, loyalty, and intentions, we wouldn't have experienced the craziest four years of life that anyone could imagine, but you know what they say – everything happens for a reason.

CHAPTER ONE

I couldn't have been happier for my man. His career was finally taking off, and he was booking shows in different states. His hard work was paying off, and these big steps forward were the moments he had been working so hard for. From long nights in the studio to going to networking events to performing in small clubs in Georgia, Cam was doing everything he could to gain exposure, and he was finally getting some big breaks. His small club bookings turned into bigger club performances which turned into opening up shows for some of the country's biggest rappers. He no longer had to beg people to take a copy of his mixtape because DJs had his album in heavy rotation.

As we sat in our apartment in downtown Atlanta, enjoying a rare day off, Cam's phone began to ring. It was Lew, Cam's manager. Cam stood up from the couch and quickly walked to our bedroom to take the call. After a few minutes, Cam emerged from our bedroom with a huge smile across his face.

"Babe, I'm leaving for New York!" he excitedly said after he hung up the phone from speaking to his manager. "I landed a few bookings at some venues in New York, and I need to pack up and be at the airport in a few hours."

He tackled me on to our living room couch and playfully bit the side of my neck. Chills ran down my spine and I pulled him in even closer, running my hands across his back. He smelled so good, and although I was thrilled for him, I wished we had a few more hours to enjoy together. It was rare that I had a day off from class on the same day he didn't have studio time, an interview, or an appearance. As much as I wanted to rip off his pants, I knew I needed to help him pack so he was prepared for his last-minute trip. If I left it up to him, he would pack some designer shoes and forget the necessities.

"I couldn't have done this without you," he whispered in my ear as we held each other on the couch.

I smiled and nuzzled my nose into his neck. I loved hearing those words. My support for him was always unwavering, and I'm glad he recognized that. Whether he needed me by his side at an event or to listen to his new music, I was always ready and willing to help and support.

After scooting Cam off me, I got off the couch and stepped into our walk-in closet to begin pulling a few pairs of his jeans and a couple of shirts from his side of the closet.

"Cam, what exactly do you need for the road? I want to make sure I don't overpack for you," I shouted from the closet.

"I have about three shows, so just grab me six pairs of jeans and six shirts and I'll be straight. That should be fine for when I'm not on stage," he answered as he sat down on the bed and scrolled through his phone.

Through the reflection of our large closet mirror, I watched Cam browse through his phone, and I couldn't help but wonder how many bitches he may have been alerting regarding his upcoming trip. Within a matter of seconds, I dismissed those wandering thoughts from my mind and continued to pack, admittedly a bit sad I couldn't tag along. I could tag along if I wanted to, but I had a commitment to school, and missing class was a no go. Being with him on the road would be amazing, but I really wanted to finish my degree. So, Cam would have to hit the road without me. Then again, babysitting him wasn't my idea of fun, and I had a feeling that's exactly what I would've been doing if I joined him on the road. The groupies, the afterparties, the adoring fans – that's what I'd face, night in and night out, and although I'm a confident chick, I didn't know if those were circumstances I would've necessarily enjoyed.

After neatly folding Cam's clothes into his suitcase and making sure he had all the toiletries he needed, I closed his luggage and placed it by our front door.

"Cam, babe, you gotta go. You're going to be late," I

reminded him as I walked back to our bedroom where he was grabbing his charger from the wall.

"I'm going, I'm going," he said as he rose to his feet, quickly placing his phone in his back pocket. "Gimme a kiss before I go. I'll miss you," he said as he lifted me up and hoisted my legs around him.

As my hands were wrapped around his neck, I quickly glanced at my watch and realized I had a few minutes to break him off before he hit the road. After all, I wanted to give my man something to remember before he left for New York. I gently slid off Cam's body, and as he moved toward the door, I pulled him by the back of his shirt and turned him around. Caught off guard by my gesture, seemingly wondering why I was stopping him after I had just tried to rush him out of the house, I then dropped to my knees, unzipped his pants, and slowly pulled his jeans to his feet. Cam broke into a huge grin, quickly realizing I was about to suck every drop of cum from his dick. I pulled out his dick and swallowed all ten inches until it grew rock hard in my throat. Cam moaned, totally not expecting me to top him off before he left. I knew he loved this shit. I could make him cum faster than he'd ever care to admit. As he stood there and thrusted his dick deeper into my throat, he then took my hand and guided it to his balls. I squeezed them just right while his dick swirled around the back of my mouth.

"Damn, Babe. You feel so fuckin' good," he groaned.

Cam gripped my long hair and pulled me into his dick, back and forth, back and forth. I let my tongue swirl around the head, working my way down his shaft, licking every inch with pleasure.

Seconds later, without warning, he busted in my mouth. As I tried to swallow, a few drops of cum escaped my lips. As he looked down, I took his finger, swiped it across my lips, and licked the cum clean.

"You a freak, Jaz, you know that?" he laughed, loving every second of our last-minute rendezvous.

As he zipped up his pants and adjusted his belt, I stood up to walk him to the door, but for real this time. I figured now was a good time to warn him about being reckless on the road.

"Be good," I said. "I'm not playin' with you, Cam," I warned in a serious tone. "Don't disrespect me on the road."

"Damn, Jaz, I won't. Give a nigga some credit. I'm not about to be doin' no crazy shit, just performing and chillin'."

His response sounded good, but I believed his track record with turning away bitches wasn't too hot.

"I'll see you next week, Baby," he sweetly said before giving me one last kiss. Then, he closed the door behind him, with his luggage in tow, ready to take on New York.

***

It had been three days since Cam left for New York and

I was already bored. Having him around, even if we were just laying around or grabbing a bite to eat, was fun in itself. Needless to say, life was dull when he was away for his shows. I missed my man, and I could tell he missed me too because we Facetimed at least five times each day. On day one, he showed me his stage set-up for his first show and gave me a quick tour of his dressing room.

"Babe, ya nigga is big time! They got me Skittles and Perrier. You know that shit is my favorite," he excitedly said as he zoomed in on his modest table of goodies in his dressing room.

I could tell he was excited, and I almost wished I ditched class to experience this with him. In a few more days, he would be home, and I was already looking forward to him being back in my arms. In the meantime, however, I wanted to stay distracted. So, I gave my little sister a call.

"Brit, what's up?" I asked after she picked up my call on the first ring. "Do you want to go to dinner tonight?" I asked, hopeful that my little sister would agree to be my date.

"I'm sorry, Jaz, I can't. I'm going to Liz's house to help her pack, remember? She's moving to Texas next week," my sister said.

"Oh, that's right! I forgot she's moving. Tell her I said good luck with her move, okay?"

"Okay! I'll see you this week though. Text me if you need me," my sister said before hanging up the phone. I remembered Brittany telling me that her friend, Liz, was moving, but it must have slipped my mind.

So, with no plans and very little desire to leave the house, I figured I'd enjoy some alone time at home. I walked into our bedroom and threw on Cam's house clothes, my favorite pair of his gray sweatpants and his old black Nike hoodie. Before crawling under the covers to relax and watch a movie, I grabbed the cookie dough ice cream from the freezer, the same pint I've been saving for a quiet night like this.

"*Gone Girl* or *John Wick*," I said aloud, attempting to choose between two of my favorite movies.

I decided to go with *John Wick*, even though Cam and I have watched this movie at least 15 times, but I really wasn't in the mood for that crazy shit in *Gone Girl*. As entertaining as that movie was, I needed some sort of action flick in my life.

As the opening scene of *John Wick* appeared on the screen, I started scrolling through my phone.

"I wonder what he's up to," I murmured while signing into Cam's Instagram account. Cam had no clue I had access to his Instagram, but he didn't need to know, either. Recently, I figured out his password and I checked his account from time to time to see if he was up to no good. The only thing I ever really saw were some DMs with his boys about some dumb memes, messages from club promoters, and a few thirsty messages he sent to girls occasionally. This time, his timeline was dry as hell with pictures of the same old shit —

dudes flexing in front of exotic cars knowing damn well they don't have a pot to piss in and the usual faux-model chicks vacationing in Dubai or some foreign country, hoping for a Birkin or enough money to pay their car note. Then, I decided to read through his DMs, the holy grail of any man's Instagram. They may have been boring in the past, but I certainly hoped it would stay that way. The first message that popped up was between Cam and one of his friend's ex-girlfriends, Zoe. Zoe had been messing with a member of Deelos, the popular three-man rap group, yet there was Cam, shooting his shot in her DMs.

Come by my hotel. I'm tryna see you.

So much for missing me and so much for uneventful DMs. This nigga couldn't wait to be far enough to creep in a different city, but from the looks of their conversation, she shot down his request. After turning him down though, she quickly offered to hook Cam up with her friend, Crystal.

Imma come through with Crystal. She been eyein' you for a while. I just talked to her and she said she'll come through to see you tonight.

"Come through to see you tonight? The fuck is this shit?" I said to myself, baffled as fuck by their conversation. Feeling a mix of sheer rage and nausea, I exited out of Cam's DMs. Zoe knew damn well he was in a relationship, yet she was offering up my man to her hoe-ass friend, Crystal. Zoe and I have crossed paths in the past due to mutual friends. In fact, she recently saw Cam and I when we were out for sushi, yet this bitch had the nerve to write Cam and act as if I didn't exist. Crystal's ass was always traveling all over the place, one day in Atlanta and the next in L.A. Apparently, though, she was in New York and acting like the groupie bitch I heard she was. I never cared what she did, but I started to care when it involved my man.

I was furious, but Cam was on stage at the time so I couldn't phone him to call him out on his shit, and I knew I couldn't call my sister because she was already tired of Cam's antics. So, I sat in bed and let this shit fester, constantly checking his DMs to see if I could find anything out about his night or supposed rendezvous with Crystal.

A few hours later, my movie came to an end and I was still clueless about Cam and this chick.

Did they fuck?

Was he feeling this girl?

Why the hell is he doing this shit?

Things have been so good with us. How could he?

A million questions swirled around my mind, and the unknown about his evening was driving me insane. I had no idea when Cam's show would end, and I knew he was headed to the club after his show for a booked appearance. So, with no other choice, knowing I didn't want to have a text conversation with him about my findings, I put my phone on the charger, closed my eyes, and tried to get some sleep.

CHAPTER TWO

As the sun peeked through the clouds, bursts of light made their way through our large bedroom windows. I lazily rolled to my side, reached for my phone on my nightstand, and began checking my messages. I had five missed calls from Cam and a few unread texts from him, too. This nigga had the nerve to say he was going to bed right after he got home from the club. Yeah, when pigs fly.

Before calling him back, I needed to get my thoughts together. So, I signed back into his Instagram account to find out if anything transpired with Crystal.

Shorty was ready. I tore her ass up!

There it was, a message from Cam to his boy, bragging about fucking Crystal.

Part of me wanted to cuss his ass out, leave our apartment, and never look back. Another part of me wanted to go at Crystal's neck and her loose-ass friend, Zoe, who set up this entire thing. I didn't know where to direct my anger, but after a few seconds, I decided to make Zoe my first target. I searched for her profile on Instagram, clicked the "message" button, and proceeded to write her dumb ass.

Bitch, you knew Cam had a girl. Why the fuck you set your friend up with my man? You got a lot of nerve, bitch.

I sent that DM with a quickness and stood by, awaiting her response.

To my surprise, she read my message within a few minutes.

"Typical. The bitch probably lives on Instagram," I muttered under my breath.

Shit, I ain't sleep with Cam. Crystal did. Be mad at yo nigga! He hasn't put no ring on your finger, so at the end of the day, your relationship don't mean shit!"

I hated to admit it, but the bitch was right. Her message stung like a million bees, but she told no lies. Cam and I were in a relationship but exclusivity was something I clearly honored, and he didn't. He wasn't my husband, and from the looks of it, he was barely my man. I didn't bother writing Zoe back. There was no point. I couldn't argue with facts, so I closed the app and slammed my phone on the bed.

As I paced our apartment, my anger only deepened, and my thoughts spiraled.

How could I be so stupid to think he would be faithful?

Do I mean anything to this nigga?

Did I ever mean anything to him?

I can't deal with this shit!

I picked up my phone from the bed, ready to make my next move. "Siri, call Cam!" I shouted into my phone, ready to let this nigga have it. Enough was enough, and I couldn't hold my anger inside anymore. There I was, faithful and foolish at home while this dude was sticking his dick into God knows who in New York. Well, no more. He could have these hoes because I was done. I've always said that I never caught Cam in the act, but this was basically the same thing. He admitted what he did, and there was no denying it.

As my phone rang, Cam answered on the second ring.

"Hey, Babe! I've been trying to reach you and –," Cam happily said before I cut his ass off.

"Nigga, shut the fuck up! So, you fuckin' Crystal? Who else you fuckin' on the road? Matter of fact, don't answer that. I'm done with you. This relationship is motherfuckin' over, so you can have every last one of these hoes. After all, there ain't no ring on my finger. I ain't shit to you!" I shouted in the phone, feeling a major sense of relief as I let him know his ass was caught.

"Jaz, what the fuck you talkin' about? I ain't do shit! You always accusing me of something, and I'm tired of this shit!"

"Oh, yeah? Interesting, because I read your DMs. 'Tore that ass up', huh?" I said as the other end of the phone fell silent. "Cam, we're done. This is the life you want, so go live it.

I'm through with your ass," I said, hanging up the phone.

He called my phone for the next 30 minutes straight until I finally turned my phone off. I didn't want to hear a gotdamn thing he had to say.

"He hasn't put no ring on your finger, so at the end of the day, your relationship don't mean shit!"

Crystal's words rang in my head like a blaring alarm clock. Cam and I may have been exclusive, and we may have moved in together, but without a ring, our relationship status no longer felt significant.

I stormed back to our bedroom and began throwing things in my luggage. I didn't know where to start packing, because our closet was full of my clothes, shoes, and bags, but I figured I could grab what I needed and then come back later for more. I picked up my black leather Chanel boy bag, threw it into my luggage, and felt angry all over again. Nearly every new bag and pair of shoes in my closet was a gift from Cam, sometimes given as a random surprise or as a guilt gift. The man may have been an asshole at times, but he sure did know what the hell to buy me to put a smile on my face.

"Man, fuck this shit!" I shouted as I slammed down my purse and walked to the kitchen, temporarily abandoning my packing task. Cam wasn't returning home for another three days, so I figured I'd cook a big ass meal for myself, dirty up the kitchen, and dip. He left a mess of my heart, so I decided to leave a mess of his kitchen, not exactly an even exchange but it was a start toward making me feel better.

Opening the refrigerator, I took out some salted butter and a small container of heavy cream. Then, I walked to our pantry and grabbed some sea salt, ground pepper, and fresh nutmeg. Penne alfredo was my favorite comfort meal, and this dish was about to give me some temporary relief.

As the butter melted over low heat in the small saucepan, my mind flashed to Cam fucking that girl in his hotel room or wherever the hell they had sex. I imagined his body on top of hers, fucking her the same way he fucks me.

"Ain't no way he used a condom, either," I muttered as I envisioned them rolling around in bed.

Suddenly, I was no longer hungry, and I just wanted to leave our apartment. My favorite comfort meal wouldn't erase these thoughts from my mind, and I knew I couldn't heal, let alone feel less angry, in a place that serves as a constant reminder to my failed relationship. I realized I would have to tell Brittany what happened because her condo was the only place I wanted to go. Even though she was going to be pissed about this, there was no where else I wanted to be than with my sister. So, I reluctantly turned on my phone to dial Brittany's number. Within seconds of turning on my phone, it began to ring. An unknown number appeared on the screen.

"Hello?" I answered, instantly regretting answering this unknown call.

"Baby, just listen to me, please!" Cam pleaded from the

other end.

"You know what? I'm going to stay on the line because I'm dying to hear the excuse you managed to come up with. Go ahead, Cam. I'm waiting to hear this bullshit. What've you come up with now?" I boldly asked and laughed as he began stuttering and stammering on the other end.

"Baby, I, I, I fucked up. I ain't even going to lie to you. I'm so sorry, Jaz. I know I fucked up. Please, let me make this up to you. Please," he begged, and for a split second, I wanted to cave into his apology. He sounded so sincere and even a bit scared, too, but I had to push those thoughts out of my mind and not give Cam credit for something he didn't deserve. Thankfully, I quickly pushed that compassion out of my heart, stayed strong, and didn't fall weak to his begging.

"Actions speak louder than words," I quietly reminded myself under my breath.

"Jaz, I can't hear you. What did you say? Do you forgive me? Will we be okay?" he asked in a panic.

I paused before answering. He needed to feel a twinge of anxiety, at the very least, for dragging me through this ordeal. My heart ached, and he thought a 30-second phone call, asking for forgiveness, would make this right. Well, he thought wrong.

"Nah, not this time. You really thought a quick apology over the phone was about to make me jump for joy and act like you didn't do what you did?! I'm done with you, Cam. We're done. I'm packing up and leaving. When you get home, I'll be gone. You should've thought twice before fuckin' some bitch in New York. I hope Crystal was worth it," I said, hanging up the phone and turning my ringer on silent.

I meant what I said. I was done with Camron.

***

I spent the night at Cam's apartment, no longer considering it my home. I was hesitant to tell Brittany what happened, so I figured I could buy myself a night before telling her what transpired between Cam and me. After taking a quick shower, I threw on some clothes and decided to watch a little bit of TV before heading to Brittany's condo. The day dragged on, and each minute felt like an hour, no matter how much I tried to distract myself. About 15 minutes into a rerun of some trashy reality show, I heard the knob jiggle on our front door. Cam wasn't to return home for another few days, and although our high-rise was protected by a code system, I feared someone slid past that and was trying to break in. After all, Cam was more well-known, especially in Atlanta, and I wouldn't put it past someone in this scheming-ass town to break into our place. I jolted from the couch, fear stricken, and quietly tip-toed to the kitchen to grab a knife. We didn't have a gun at home, and the only weapon I had within reach was a cutting knife. It wasn't much, but I wanted to be armed with something, anything, as this person continued to fumble with the lock on the front door.

"Damnit, I knew we should've gotten a dog or at least a dead bolt," I quietly cried as I crouched in the corner of the kitchen. A few seconds later, the door opened, and I peered from the kitchen in hopes to get a good look at who was breaking into our home.

"Jaz? Jaz? Are you home?"

Cam stormed through the front door like a bat out of hell, hoping I would be home, not knowing I was ducked off in the kitchen ready to stab an intruder.

"I was just leaving," I flatly said, rising to my feet and setting the knife down on the counter. I then coldly walked back to the bedroom to grab my luggage.

"Jaz, please, just listen. I left my tour early. I left all that shit behind. I couldn't risk losing you. Please, just hear me out," he begged, and for a moment, I thought I saw Cam tear up, but I wasn't trying to stare into his eyes long enough to find out. His shitty ass apology over the phone didn't win me over and his tears certainly wouldn't either.

Ignoring his pleas, I picked up my luggage and stormed past him.

"Nigga, goodbye. You and these tired-ass apologies. Shit's old, Cam. Real old," I said, never looking in his direction.

He quickly ran in front of me and blocked the front

door with his arms, refusing to let me leave.

"Get the fuck out the way, Cam. I'm not playin' with you," I demanded, gritting my teeth as this fool was sweating and shaking, standing in front of the door.

"Jaz, if I could take this shit back, I would in a fuckin' second. I love you, and you were right," he stuttered, seemingly too flustered to speak clearly.

"I was right about what?" I demanded, quickly regretting giving him the opportunity to explain himself yet wanting to hear the ways in which he knew he messed up. My ego was shot, so I figured I deserved a bit of groveling.

"The ring, us, everything. You were right, and I want to do this the right way."

I had never seen Cam look that way before. His hands were trembling and sweat beads continued to form on his chocolate-complected forehead. Normally, when we argue, he turns the tables and makes shit out to be my fault, but this time was different. He was visibly upset with himself and couldn't find the right words to express himself. His hands continued to shake as he feebly attempted to speak.

"Jaz," he said, slowly kneeling at my feet. "I love you, and I want to spend forever with you. Just us. No more games. I'm serious. Will you be my wife?" he asked as he fumbled to position a small black velvet box in front of my eyes.

As Cam opened the box, I was taken aback by the outrageous, princess-cut diamond and platinum band that rested so perfectly in the velvet box. How this man managed to cancel his tour, buy me a ring, and propose before I left our apartment was beyond me. For once, his apology went above and beyond a bag or pair of shoes. This man was offering a commitment to forever, and I was stunned.

I was lost in my thoughts and frozen in shock when he popped the question again. "Please, Jasmine. Will you be my wife? I love you, and I promise to never hurt you again."

I took a deep breath, kneeled in front of Cam, and searched his eyes, hoping to find the answers to the questions buzzing around my mind. My brain escaped me, and I couldn't manage to speak the thoughts on my heart. Although this ring was everything I ever wanted from him, and his proposal was everything I ever wanted to hear, I still had a laundry list of shit I wanted to scream in his face.

Oh, now you love me?

Now you don't want to lose me?

All of a sudden, you're ready for marriage?

Why did you do this, Cam? Why?

As thought after thought piled up in my mind, I remained silent, too overcome with emotion to speak.

As we stood there staring at each other, Cam pulled me into him kissed me on the cheek. He slowly pulled away and lightly kissed my lips. Now staring at each other again, he put his hands around my face and pulled me for another kiss, this time deeper. His DMs, the situation with Crystal, his lies –

everything escaped my mind and all I could think about was how much I loved this man, how much I wanted him, and how badly I wanted us to work out.

As we kissed, Cam laid me down on the living room rug and slowly pulled away. He began unbuttoned my jeans, and he slid them off my body, never breaking his stare. My pussy was soaking wet in anticipation. I caught a glimpse of the ring in my peripheral vision and couldn't believe this was happening, whatever "this" was. Cam gently turned me around, laid on top of me, pulled my panties to the side, and slid his dick inside of me while gripping my neck. He knew exactly what I liked, and although my emotions were all over the place, I didn't want him to stop.

"I love you, Jasmine," he whispered in my ear as he went deeper, giving me every inch of his dick.

"I love you too, Baby," I moaned.

This is how it always went – we fuss, we fight, we fuck – but this argument ended in a proposal, something he's never done or even discussed with me.

After ten minutes of slow, deep strokes, I told Cam to put his dick in my mouth. I wanted to taste him, and I lowkey loved how it felt after he had been deep inside of me. I sat on his face as he licked my clit, and his dick motioned in and out of the back of my throat. Moments later, we climaxed together, and Cam collapsed next to me as if he just ran a marathon. The room fell silent and time seemed to stand still for a moment.

"Jasmine?" Cam finally said. "Do you forgive me? Do you want to be my wife?"

"I can't believe you left your tour!" I exclaimed. "Was Lew pissed?" I asked, brushing right past his questions.

"Damnit, Jasmine. I'm asking you to be my wife. Are you listening? I love you. Please, make me the happiest man alive and marry me."

I paused for a moment, already knowing my reply yet enjoying the fact that he was squirming a bit. Shit, I've squirmed plenty of times in this relationship. He could wait a few minutes for my answer.

"Yes, Cam, I will marry you," I said as I cracked a smile.

"My girl said yes!" Cam screamed, jumping to his feet to grab the ring to put on my finger.

"How did you find the time to buy this ring?" I asked in disbelief as I held my hand out to admire my new piece of jewelry.

"Everything you said to me, before you hung up on me, really got to me. You were right, and I knew I had to come correct if I was going to fix this. So, I called my jeweler in New York, and he designed a ring for me that day. Lew picked it up, and I flew home on the next available flight."

Stunned by Cam's response and the fact that Lew didn't stop him from leaving, I flashed the biggest smile and gave Cam a giant hug.

"Baby, I promise to do right by you. This is a new beginning for us," he assured me, and although he said everything I've always wanted to hear, I couldn't help but wonder if this was the real deal or a temporary chess move to keep me in his life.

CHAPTER THREE

As we pulled up to the giant white building in the center of the city, I couldn't help but notice the weather. The clouds were dark grey, almost black, and the sky looked as if it was ready to open up for a downpour. I don't know if the rain was an omen, but I once read that rain on a wedding day is good luck. Some would have said Cam and I need all the luck we could get, but I thought otherwise. Our relationship was in a great place – no fights, no cheating, and no dysfunction. This was the relationship I envisioned, and I was happy as hell to know that Cam was becoming the man I always knew he'd be. Exactly one month after his proposal, we found ourselves making our way to the courthouse to get married, hand in hand, ready to commit to forever. This was the moment I was waiting for with him, to be his wife, to belong to each other and no one else, to have and to hold, through sickness and health. Granted, a courthouse wedding wasn't part of my childhood dream, but I no longer cared. The commitment to one another and the follow through mattered most, and the best part of it all was that this wasn't forced. I never nagged Cam to pick a date, and I never begged him to meet me at the altar. In fact, Cam wanted to set a date and set a date fast. His sense of urgency showed me he was serious about this commitment, and I was down to get married as soon as we could, too. I happily obliged, despite our less than lavish venue.

After finding a parking spot at the front of the building, we made our way up the narrow, seemingly never-ending concrete steps of the courthouse. Cam looked at me adoringly with his almond-shaped brown eyes and said, "Baby, I can't wait for you to be my wife." Those words were music to my ears, and I was on cloud nine. Suddenly, the courthouse looked like the most magical place in the world. I had my man, and we were about to have forever, together.

No one was at the courthouse with us, it was only me and Cam. I mean, no one supported our relationship, and in retrospect, I can't really blame them. For a while, we were unstable as fuck with random moments of stability. I could blame his job and his industry, but Cam was a grown ass man who could've made better decisions despite the constant temptation. He didn't always make better decisions though, so our cycle was a perpetual circle of temptation, giving into temptation, begging for forgiveness, and crazy make-up sex. I don't know if it was blind love or the hopeless belief that this man would change his cheating ways, but I stuck around, and we found our way to a place of committing to forever. Our love story may not have been conventional or a picture-perfect fairy tale, but it was ours, and we were about to ride this thing 'til the wheels fell off.

At 24 years old, I believed a ring meant something. This ring was more than a piece of gorgeous jewelry. This was a promise of forever. As if this beautiful engagement ring wasn't amazing in itself, I was about to be a wife, no longer a girlfriend, and I was sure that this title was going to change *everything*. No bitch could dare tell me again that my relationship didn't mean shit. Admittedly, I felt a sense of pride as I walked up those stairs to the courthouse. To all the hoes who thought I didn't mean shit to Cam or doubted our relationship, this wedding was a giant fuck you to all of them. I had my man, I had my ring, and I was about to be a wife, *his wife*. This ring meant I could kiss all the bullshit goodbye because this marriage was about to be our fresh start, and no one could come in between us. I know how the saying goes, though – fool me once, shame on you, fool me twice, shame on me. Honestly, he fooled me more than twice, but deep down I believed he was capable of change and being a faithful man. Our ups outweighed the downs, and I believed in him. I believed in us, and I knew a lasting marriage requires more than one willing and committed participant, and no amount of money or nice bags and shoes could comfort you in the place of a loving, faithful partner.

Memories of my childhood flashed before my eyes as we walked through the large oak-finished doors of the county courthouse. I thought about my mom, the most resilient woman I've ever known. She raised Brittany and I, alone, and as a single mother, her trials and tribulations were magnified because she was a one-person team. Although she did a phenomenal job of raising me and my sister, I knew I wanted a different family dynamic. I wanted a husband, I wanted to have kids together, and I wanted to raise a strong, healthy family together. People do shit backwards nowadays by having a baby first and then hoping for a stable, happy marriage. Cam and I were breaking generational curses before our very own eyes, and I could tell he felt a sense of pride about this level of commitment, too. After our engagement, our relationship took a turn for the best and I saw visions of a healthy marriage become more realistic than ever.

Truth be told, I was surprised that he didn't use a flashy ring as a means for me to forgive him so he could go back to fucking whomever he wanted. He actually followed through on his word and set a date. Not only that, but he proudly told everyone about our engagement. His label threw us an intimate engagement party, and a few well-known magazines published a story about Cam's proposal, conveniently leaving out the part about him cheating. Well, the day finally arrived where we would meet at the altar, and we weren't turning back.

We entered the courthouse, barely escaping the rain. Cam opened the double doors for me, and we proceeded to go through security. My dream of wearing a beautiful gown was replaced by my reality of casual clothes and a pair of gold Jimmy Choo heels from my closet. Cam looked so sexy though. He wore jeans and a simple t-shirt with a few pieces of flashy jewelry, now that he could afford real jewelry, and I wore a simple, form-fitting white dress that came above my knees. After passing through security, we approached a small waiting area. There were other couples at the courthouse, and they all looked so happy.

"That's about to be us," I joyfully marveled under my breath, admittedly in disbelief, too. Although I was happy, I also had the jitters.

Are these jitters normal?

Is this too soon?

Will Cam stay faithful?

Doubts crept into my mind and manifested into fear. Cam must have noticed my apprehension because he grabbed my hand, gave me a kiss on the cheek, and stood a bit closer as we waited our turn. A few moments later, a man in what appeared to be a security uniform instructed us to walk to the second floor. As Cam and I exited the elevator, now on the second floor, a short, thin man, presumably the priest, kindly waved at us, prompting Cam and I to walk toward the alter.

Joining hands, we walked down the aisle together and stood in front of the large, rustic-looking wooden arch. The designated priest was a few feet in front of us with a smile on his face, prompting us to exchange our vows.

"Camron," the priest said, directing his attention to my future husband. "Do you take Jasmine to be your wedded wife, to live together in marriage? Do you promise to love, comfort, honor, and keep her? For better or worse, for richer or poorer, in sickness and in health?

"For richer or for poorer," he said, repeating after the priest and seeming to genuine mean every word. I searched Cam's eyes for any hint of nervousness or doubt. Instead, he exuded peace, a peace I had never seen in him.

While Cam recited his vows, my mind drifted for a moment, and I began thinking countless thoughts about what it would mean to be a wife, his wife.

I'm going to be an incredible wife to this man.

I will submit to him, and I know he will lead us in the right direction.

This is the start of a beautiful forever.

The priest's voice became a bit louder, noticeably excited that we were nearing the end of our vows, about to officially become husband and wife. I looked at Cam, and he was still smiling. His eyes met mine, and for a moment, I thought he was going to cry, but no tears ever fell.

"You are now husband and wife," the priest announced.

"Camron, you may kiss your bride," he concluded. Cam gently grabbed my face, pulled me in, and kissed my lips.

"Forever," he whispered as our foreheads rested against one another.

***

The rush of getting married was more intense than I imagined, certainly more powerful than any argument or make-up sex session we've had. Cam and I walked out of the courthouse, hand in hand, unsure of where to go or what to do, but we knew we wanted to celebrate.

"Let's go get something to eat," he excitedly said. "We can't just go home! Shit, we just got married. We gotta celebrate!"

I laughed and agreed. Even after something as serious as getting married, Cam always knew how to lighten the mood and make me laugh.

The rain had subsided, so we hopped into his Range, buckled our seatbelts, and headed to Tony's, a nearby steakhouse which happened to be our favorite restaurant. It was a bit early for dinner, only 5 in the afternoon, but we didn't care. This was the best day of our lives, and we wanted to enjoy every moment.

As Cam turned on to the main road of Tony's, we noticed valet had yet to set up. So, Cam pulled into the nearby lot to park the car. Suddenly, his phone rang. In my peripheral vision, I saw the name on the screen – *Mama*.

"Hey, Mama!" Cam said as he answered his phone.

Within a matter of seconds, Cam's mood went from ecstatic to miserable as he listened to his mother on the other end.

"Mama, I'm a grown man. You need to trust me. I know what I'm doing, okay? I love you," he finally said before hanging up the phone.

I didn't even have to ask because I already knew what that conversation was about. His mom never liked me. In fact, she hated me, and she knew today was the day we were going to the courthouse. According to her, no one was good enough for her son, but I never quite understood how she could hate me when she never took the time to get to know me. Plus, I met Cam before he had anything to his name. I loved the hell out of him when all he could afford was sticky notes for cards and flowers from the grocery store. She couldn't possibly think I was a gold-digger, and if she did, that was one misconception I didn't care to dispel because I met Cam when he slept on his grandmama's couch. Ain't no way anyone was about to tell me I was in it for the money and fame because everybody knows he couldn't offer me shit when we met. Shit, he couldn't offer me a gotdamn thing for months. I was the established one, not him, and I never held it over his head and I never assumed there would be some sort of payout in the long run. Well, everyone seemed to know those fun facts except for his skeptical mother.

"Let's go, Jaz," he mumbled under his breath, prompting me to get out of the car.

As I stepped out of the car and met Cam by the driver's side door, we proceeded to walk into Tony's together. This time, however, unlike our time at the courthouse, we weren't hand in hand, and the excitement from earlier this afternoon was apparently gone. His mother robbed us of our celebratory moment when she opened her mouth to talk shit about me and our decision to get married at the courthouse. She was welcomed to come, but she refused, so it's not like she could have been upset about a lack of invite. As we walked into the restaurant, I silently prayed that this ordeal with Cam's mom wasn't an indication of what was to come.

CHAPTER FOUR

"It's now or never," I mumbled under my breath while holding Cam's iPad.

As I sat in our apartment, the apartment we shared, I had a nagging gut feeling to check this nigga's iCloud, and I couldn't ignore it. A woman's intuition is nothing to play with. We can't ignore it, even if we try. This feeling just sits in the pit of our stomach like a 50-pound weight until we finally act on it. Some women stay quiet until the time is right, and other women strike when they feel like it. I was a combination of the two, sometimes lashing out and other times waiting to attack like a lion on its prey.

It had been a few weeks since we tied the knot, and Cam was wrapping up a major tour for the next two months, as he was the opening act for a well-known rapper. So, I knew around when he would finally fall asleep after performing and partying. The sun was barely peeking from the clouds, and there was no doubt in my mind this nigga wouldn't be awake at 7 in the morning which meant it was the perfect time to do some detective work. Part of me wanted my gut feeling to be wrong, but deep down I knew he was doing some shit behind my back. He was on the last leg of his tour, traveling from Pennsylvania to New York, and I figured I had enough time to get my shit together and leave before he got back if I happened to find anything in his iCloud.

With a little bit of guess work, it took no more than 15 seconds to break into his iCloud from my iPad.

Easy work.

I knew he'd choose his birthday as his password. Simple-minded ass. Isn't it common knowledge to *not* choose your birthday for your password? At this point, there was no going back. I took a deep breath, clicked on his messages, and started to read each text, one by one.

I stay fuckin bitches raw, but I'm supposed to be married. I ain't shit LOL.

Yo! Last night, I fucked that famous bitch from "Lust and Music."

These bitches just wait for me after my show. Too easy. Didn't even know the bitch's name last night. She sucked my dick and dipped.

With every word I read, my heart fell deeper into my chest.

"This motherfucker! How could he?" I screamed.

I couldn't stop reading his messages. If I was going to

search through his iCloud, I wanted to read everything and not have any unanswered questions. Even though I had a shitty feeling about what he was doing on tour, reading those texts still hurt like hell. This nigga was bragging and laughing with his friends about cheating when we literally just got married. He didn't even have the decency to attempt to be faithful. The ink barely dried on our marriage certificate and this nigga was fuckin bitches, raw, nonetheless. Two fuckin months of marriage and he couldn't even try not to cheat. He was on a multi-city tour, and after reading those messages there was no doubt in my mind he fucked someone new after every show.

I read every message from the lame ass "I love you" texts he sent to his mama to the "what's up bighead" texts he sent to a bunch of no-name hoes. I had to move quickly because it was nearing 8 am and I knew his manager would wake him up in a bit to grab food before heading out to his show in New York.

After I read through his texts, I clicked on his photo albums. To add insult to injury, Cam saved nudes of a chick, a chick who looked strangely familiar. After a few seconds of racking my brain as to who this woman could be, I remembered that she was from some ratchet ass reality show. Her name was Fortune, the mannish-looking chick from Louisiana, and she was on all fours, ass naked, in my man's iPad. Funny, dudes never seem to try you with someone badder than you. It's always some bum-ass hoe.

My blood was boiling, and a million angry thoughts swirled around my mind. Hot tears formed in the corners of my eyes, and all I could do was put my head in my hands and sob. I gave this man my life, my entire heart, and he was making an ass out of me while I was loyal as fuck to him. Our vows hardly meant anything to Cam. Shit, he could've given me a gotdamn disease. Thankfully, I just got tested a few days ago during my annual, so I knew I was clean.

I took a deep breath and slowly wiped the tears from my eyes. I couldn't just sit at this computer desk all day, but the lump in my throat and pain in my chest made it hard to move. I knew I'd deal with his ass at some point, but as for Fortune, the world wide web was about to catch a glimpse of her loose pussy. Since she wanted to send pictures to a married man, knowing full well he had a wife, she was quickly added to my shit list, too.

Click and submit

Before logging out of Cam's iCloud, I leaked Fortune's pictures to one of the biggest urban blogs on the web. The bitch clearly wanted attention, so I figured I'd give her ass a head start.

***

Fortune's nudes spread throughout the internet faster

than her legs spread for Cam. When I leaked her photos and more websites began reposting, I thought I would feel some sort of joy, but I didn't. I was numb inside, my heart was cold, and people dragging her on the internet for being a smut didn't make me feel any better. Then again, I also didn't give a fuck that she faced potential humiliation, either. She should've thought twice before sending pictures to Cam.

Cam may have been dumb as fuck for creating such an easy to guess password, but he was smart enough to know how Fortune's pictures hit the internet. Like clockwork, Cam woke up around 8 am, and word must have traveled fast because I had 18 missed calls and 15 text messages by 8:15. The texts started out sweet, as if he was trying to play it cool, but by the 10th missed call, that nigga was losing his mind.

Hey, babe. I hope you slept well. I love you.

Wifey, I miss you.

Jaz, where you at? Answer your Facetime, Babe.

Jaz, hello?

?????

Stop playin' and answer the damn phone.

With every text message, all I could do was sit in disbelief and wonder how the fuck this man could propose to me and marry me only to cheat on me a few weeks later. The nerve of him to act so concerned because I wasn't picking up the phone. He should've been that pressed a few weeks ago when he was getting fucked and sucked by women other than his wife, clearly acting like a single man in these streets. Answering his calls was not on my agenda, not now and not anytime soon. My mind was made up – *I was leaving*. No, really. This time, I was done, done.

That morning, I continued to ignore Cam's calls. Eventually, he stopped texting, assumedly because his ass didn't know what to say. I bet he wondered if he should play dumb, act fake concerned as to why I wasn't answering, or just be a dickhead. Somewhere around the 30th missed call, my phone died which was a blessing in disguise because I could no longer stay miserably distracted by his incessant messages. So, I finally mustered up the strength to take a shower and get ready to face the day. As much as I wanted to curl up on the couch and cry the day away, I refused to be a weak ass bitch over a nigga that clearly didn't deserve my tears.

I drew myself a piping hot shower, stepped inside, and let the water fall down my back. For a moment, I forgot about the pain of his betrayal and started thinking about my upcoming assignments for school. I had two end-of-semester projects due soon, and I was actually excited about turning them in. You see, Cam didn't marry some basic chick who loved him for the wrong reasons. I had goals and dreams, and I put my dreams to work regardless of his status and growing career. With only one year left of dental school, I was looking forward to working in an established practice and building for our futures. Well, my future, because Cam was no longer in my picture of forever.

After washing my body from head to toe and thoroughly rinsing off, I turned off the water, carefully stepped out of the shower, and wrapped a giant bath towel around my chest. As much as I tried to get him off my mind, memories of him were everywhere I turned. When Cam and I moved in together, we went shopping for house stuff, and I remember picking out our bath towels together. He wanted grey, and I wanted white. He caved and we went home with the white towels I had my eye on. He always let me win, except this time I felt like I was losing everything – my pride, my heart, and my husband. The same bathroom counter where those white towels sat perfectly folded was the same counter he sat me on to eat my pussy before he left for tour. Memories were everywhere, and they were hard to ignore.

Determined to snap out of it, I walked to our walk-in-closet, picked out my favorite pair of distressed boyfriend jeans and a simple black T-shirt and got dressed. Toast, a delicious local breakfast spot, was just a few blocks from our apartment, so I figured I would use today to get my mind together, eat a good meal, and pack up my shit before Cam arrives home tomorrow evening.

I was serious – *I was done with Camron.*

Thankfully, his tour gave me the time and space to gather my necessities and stay elsewhere until I had a game plan as to where I would go. For now, I just wanted to eat, pack a few things, and get the fuck out without giving him a chance to talk me into staying. He was good at that and he knew it. He knew what to say and what to do to convince me not to leave, but what the fuck could he say at this point? Those texts said it all and so did Fortune's pictures. As I finished getting ready, I decided to charge my phone. I knew my mom would panic if she tried to call me and my phone went straight to voicemail. While my phone charged, I pulled my hair into a tight ballerina bun and applied mascara and dab of lip gloss.

"Ugh, 16%," I murmured as I grabbed my phone and left our apartment, regretting not charging my phone sooner.

***

Toast was relatively quiet that day with only a few customers inside. I spotted a family of four, a few couples, and an older gentleman dining alone. I didn't want to see anyone I knew, so this desolate atmosphere suited my mood just fine.

"Table for one, please," I said to the hostess as she led me to a quiet table in the corner of the restaurant. Peace, quiet, and a good meal, exactly what I needed on a dreadful morning.

I already knew what I wanted to eat – avocado toast and an egg white omelet with spinach and mushrooms. When the waitress approached my table, I placed my order and started checking my messages as I waited for my food to arrive. Of course, Camron's messages overwhelmed my inbox.

I can't fuckin concentrate if shit ain't right with us! Answer the phone. Please, Jasmine!

You're my wife, and I love you! Please call me. Please!

Camron's messages were latent with begging and pleading, and I felt a slight surge of power knowing the ball was in my court. I've worried about this nigga for nights on end, so I hardly felt any guilt for his mini tantrum and meltdown.

Against my initial feelings, though, I decided to reply.

Fuck you. Go ask Fortune to help you concentrate. Ask her to get down on her knees again for you, Cam.

He responded within seconds, and a wave of panic surged through my body.

I'm coming home, Jaz. Fuck this tour. I've left my tour once, and you know I'll do it again. I'm leaving New York and coming home to you. I need to talk to you. I love you! Give me a chance to explain! It ain't like that!

So much for my game plan of breakfast and packing. Moments later, my food arrived, and I decided to take my time and enjoy my meal. A few seconds later, I received a message from Lew, Cam's road manager.

Jasmine, please call Camron. He's a wreck. His final show is tonight, and if he misses this show, he's going to get sued which means I get sued, too. Call him. Please. For me.

I loved Cam's road manager. He was like family, but I

wasn't going to call Cam, not even for him.

Lew, he should've thought about that before he stepped out on me. We're not dating anymore. We're married, and clearly I'm the only one who took our vows seriously. I'm sorry, but I'm done with him.

I finished my meal, down to the last bite, and subtly waved down my waitress to pay my bill. After leaving cash on the table, I placed my wallet back into my purse, put on my oversized black Gucci sunglasses, and walked back to our apartment to pack up and get the fuck out of there before Cam arrived home. This time, I wasn't taking any chances with him coming home early.

CHAPTER FIVE

"Hey, sissy," Brittany said as she greeted me with a hug at the front door of her condo. Her tone was latent with sadness, presumably because what I felt she felt and vice versa. We were always very much in tune with one another's emotions, and this situation was no different. She may have hated Cam, but she was still my sister, and she felt horribly for me.

"Hey, Brit," I said, heavily sighing as I closed the door behind me.

I walked inside and headed towards her second bedroom, the bedroom that used to be mine before I moved into Cam's apartment. I looked around my old bedroom and started reminiscing about the times Cam stayed with me before he got a place of his own. Life was simple back then, so many nights of takeout and movies, morning sex, and breakfast in bed. Now, we're married, and our relationship is in shambles. "Shambles" were generous. Our marriage was hanging by a string.

"Jaz? Jaz? Hello?" Brittany said, breaking my trance. "Are you hungry? I made you lunch. Come eat with me on the couch," she gently urged, handing me a plate of macaroni and cheese, greens, and short ribs. She made one of my favorite meals, and although I was heartbroken, I was certainly going to make room for this deliciousness.

I smiled and graciously took the plate of food. As Brittany and I sat on the couch and dug into the food on our plates, my phone started to buzz.

"I turned off my ringer, but I must've forgotten to turn it off vibrate," I said mid-bite.

An unrecognizable number appeared on my phone, but the area code was from Louisiana. With a sneaking suspicion of who was on the other end, I boldly answered the phone. "The fuck you want?" I rudely demanded. Brittany set her fork down, perked up, and looked at me wide-eyed. She knew it took a lot for me to lose my cool, so my harsh tone caught her by complete surprise.

"You must've been expecting my call, dirty-ass bitch," the woman on the other end barked into the phone. "You think you funny, huh? Postin' my pictures on the internet? Well, I was just callin' to inform yo stupid ass that I called the police, and I *will* be pressing charges. What you did is revenge porn, hoe, and that's a felony. How you like that?" she chuckled.

The furious woman on the other end was none other than Fortune, the butt-naked woman in Cam's phone that I just so happened to recently blast on the web.

"I have no idea what you're talking about," I sarcastically said. "Sounds like you got a problem on your hands, but that ain't got shit to do with me," I laughed in an attempt to rattle her. There was no way I was about to admit to posting her pictures online. She could've been recording our phone call for all I knew.

"Jasmine, I know it was you! And do you wanna know how I know?" Fortune asked, pausing before answering her own question. In that moment of silence, I became enraged that she knew my name.

"Honey, I didn't send those pictures to Camron. Camron *took* those pictures of me. Matter of fact, he took them on his iPhone when I spent the night in his hotel a few weeks back. It was so sweet, too. We laid up in bed, ordered room service, and one thing led to another, if you know what I mean," she snickered. "He ate my pussy. Twice. No wonder you're so sprung. He got a magical tongue. Oh, and he gave me $100, too. Such a nice gesture," she laughed.

This phone conversation was lasting too long for my liking, but this new information had me shook.

Cam took those pictures?

She stayed the night with him?

Am I the only one who understood the vows we took at the alter?

My mind was racing, and I was furious he went this far

with Fortune. The pictures were already a shot to the heart, but this dude had her in his hotel room, she spent the night, and they had sex.

"Wait, let me get this straight," I laughed, refusing to let her know that her news crushed my spirit. "You braggin' about a married man giving you $100? I guess it's true what everybody says – you really are a bum bitch. I guess them reality checks been lookin' real slim, huh?" I giggled.

The tables had turned, and for a split second, Fortune was silent.

"Well, if you ain't got shit else to say, I'm hanging up now so I can enjoy lunch with my sister. Have yourself a good day, bitch," I said, ready to end the call.

"Hold up, hold up. I didn't know the nigga was married," Fortune finally said, sounding a bit flustered. "I mean, I don't really give a fuck if he's married or not, but I ain't know is all I'm sayin'. He never mentioned a wife. Even if he did, I don't owe you shit, bitch!" she shouted, hanging up the phone.

I felt Brittany's eyes on me. She could've burned a hole in my back from the way she was glaring at me.

"She got a lot of nerve!" Brittany shouted. "I'm not married, and I've never been married, so I don't want to give you bad advice but gotdamn, Jaz. What's it going to take for you to leave this dude? You could probably get an annulment, too, because it's only been a few months."

With a heavy heart and tired mind, all I could do was sigh. While Brittany was right, that I should consider leaving Cam, deep down I wanted to save my marriage. I knew this situation wasn't healthy, but I also knew that marriage is full of ups and downs. Granted, downs shouldn't mean infidelity, drama, and disrespect, but at 24 and no solid example of a healthy marriage, I figured this was part of the process.

"Apparently, Cam took those pictures of Fortune, so now she wants to press charges against me because I hacked Cam's iCloud and had her pictures posted on the internet. Brit, I ain't even gunna lie. I don't want to go to jail over this shit. I don't know what to do!" I said, panic stricken by Fortune's threat.

"I hate to say this, but you may have to call Cam, Jaz. Have him convince Fortune to not follow through on the police report," Brittany reluctantly suggested.

I took a second and silently weighed out her suggestion. As much as I didn't want to speak to Cam, I knew he could fix this. More so, I knew he needed to fix this because this was all his fault. I may have shared those photos, but if he didn't dog me in the first place, I wouldn't have put Fortune on blast. Prior to Fortune's phone call, I had no intentions of contacting his ass, but this wasn't about him. This was about me, and I needed to make sure this problem went away and fast.

CHAPTER SIX

A few hours had passed since Fortune and I went at it over the phone, and although I knew I was going to take my sister's suggestion of calling Cam to fix this ordeal, I needed to gather my thoughts. I had nothing to say to this man, yet I was somehow at his mercy and that further pissed me off. If a bitch like Fortune was giddy over $100, I knew Cam could persuade her to drop the charges she filed, at least I hoped.

I picked up my phone and stared at the screen for a second. The man I used to jump at the chance to call was now a person I didn't want to speak to again.

"Go, Jaz. Call him," Brittany insisted, urging me to dial Cam. "This ain't about y'all. This is about you, and you need to make sure you protect yourself against this bitch. No more waiting. Handle it," my sister demanded, nodding her head toward my phone, motioning me to call.

For the last several hours, Brittany and I chilled on the couch, talked, and had a few helpings of the delicious lunch she made. During our chit chat, I realized how much I missed my sister. Even better, being with my sister distracted me from my marital issues. In the last few hours, I had more peace than I felt in the last week. Sad, but true.

As I dialed Cam's number, I realized I hadn't thought about how I would go about this or what I would say. I was emotionally exhausted from the turn of events with Cam's little jump-off, and I wasn't sure I had the energy to explode on him.

"Here goes nothing," I murmured.

The phone barely rang once before Camron answered. "Jaz, baby, I'm so glad you called. Before you say anything, I just want to tell you I love you. Don't give up on us, please," he pleaded.

His words sounded like gibberish because I've heard it all before. This was the same merry-go-round we rode when he fucked Crystal before we got engaged. The begging and pleading were no longer cute, only annoying, telling me he loved me one minute and then sticking his dick in someone else the next. That was never my picture of love.

"Nigga, shut up. I ain't call to talk about us. There is no us. I called to talk about Fortune. You know, the bitch you fucked in your hotel room? Remember her, Cam?"

"Jaz, cut it out. I ain't tryna talk about that bitch," he muttered, clearly disappointed that our conversation wasn't headed in a positive direction.

"Too bad, nigga. You got me in a mess, and I need you to get me out of it. You owe me. This is the least you could do for disrespecting our marriage. Shit, the ink is barely dry on our marriage certificate. Think about that, Cam," I retorted.

"I'll do anything," he quickly replied. "Tell me what I need to do."

"Without fucking her, convince Fortune to drop the charges on me. Can you handle that, Cam? She called me a few hours ago and told me she filed charges on me for posting her pictures online. That's a felony, and I'm not tryna get sued or go to jail. Make her drop the charges," I demanded, suddenly feeling powerful. Cam's back was against the wall, and if he wanted a chance to save our marriage, he would handle this.

"I'll do it right now. I won't do no foul shit, either. I promise, Jaz."

Before he said goodbye, I rolled my eyes and hung up the phone. I had nothing else to say to him, and I didn't want to give Cam the impression that we were okay, either. My mind wasn't even focused on our marriage. I simply wanted to know I wasn't going to get arrested, and now that Cam said he would handle it, I was able to breathe a bit easier. Within seconds, a wave of relief passed through my body, and although I couldn't trust Cam to be faithful, I felt confident he would squash this mess for me. As I waited to hear back from Camron regarding this mess with Fortune, I signed on his Instagram account.

"Want some entertainment for the evening?" I asked Brittany, managing to push out a laugh. "I'm about to look through Cam's Instagram again. Let's see how sorry this nigga really is," I said as I logged into his Instagram. Brittany hopped up from the loveseat and sat directly next to me on the couch.

Peering over my shoulder, she giggled and said, "Hell yeah! Sign on. I wanna see what his dumbass is writing to these bitches."

Camron had yet to change his password, so I had no problems logging into his account. As I made my way to his DMs, I braced myself for a flood of crude DMs between him and other bitches, but to my surprise, he left about 12 women on read, all of which were begging to meet him during his tour.

Admittedly shocked and curious by Cam's sudden change of behavior, I faced Brittany and said, "Brit, you think Cam would ever change?

"Girl, I don't know," she sighed, "but this is definitely progress because we both know he's quick to DM a bitch."

A handful of ignored DMs shouldn't have been enough to soften my heart, but it did. Cam never seemed to miss an opportunity to respond to a woman on Instagram. "Maybe he's really upset about us," I suggested. "Maybe he's scared to lose me for good."

Before Brittany had the chance to reply, my phone rang. It was Camron.

"Hey, Jaz," he said with a hint of excitement in his voice. "I just talked to ol' girl. She said she won't follow through on the report. She swore she'd dead it," he shared, and I chuckled to myself because I noticed he wouldn't even say her name. Camron was clearly walking on eggshells, as he should have been.

"How'd you convince her, Cam? You give her another $100 or you promise to eat her pussy again?" I said, not wanting Cam to think he was off the hook. "Actually, I don't care how the fuck you convinced her. I'll sleep better tonight knowing that hoe won't jeopardize my future. Goodbye, Cam," I said, hanging up the phone. Whether he called after that, I don't know, because I turned my phone off. I was determined to get peace of mind, and I knew that wouldn't be possible if he was blowing up my line.

CHAPTER SEVEN

After I hung up on Cam, I followed through with the promise I made to myself – *get peace of mind.* So, for the next three weeks, I stayed completely away from Cam and moved into Brittany's condo. My willpower was stronger than I thought, because I never caved to pick up the phone or stop by his spot, and as each day passed, I felt less devastated about Cam's recent betrayal. Between going to class, finishing school assignments and projects, and spending time with my girls, my mind was occupied in healthy ways. A good portion of my belongings still remained at Cam's, and I wasn't sure how I would go about getting them back, but for now I wanted to focus on my sanity. My clothes and what not could wait until I figured out my next move. Despite staying far away from Cam and his nonsense, he had yet to leave me alone. Since the moment I hung up on him after he told me Fortune wouldn't press charges on me, he hasn't stopped calling. Day and night, that nigga stayed leaving me long ass voicemails, voice notes, and text messages. I didn't reply to a single one, though, and why would I? For him to tell me he was sorry? Sorry is for accidents, and that nigga didn't accidentally fall into her pussy.

As I walked into the kitchen to make myself a cup of coffee, Brittany hopped up from the couch to join me.

"Morning, sis! You doin' okay today?" she asked. No matter what Brittany had going on, she always made sure to check on me. "I gotta admit," she continued. "I thought you'd take him back as soon as he handled that shit with Fortune," Brittany said. "Whether y'all mend things or not, I'm proud of you. This nigga needs to feel some fear. He needs to know you won't stick around for his shit."

I nodded and smiled. I never thought I'd avoid Cam for three weeks, but I was glad I did. In the past, with each accepted apology, I gave Cam less grounds to respect me and our relationship. I needed to shake shit up with us and shift the power back, but the truth was, I missed his ass. I wasn't sure when I would talk to him, if ever, but I told myself I would play it by ear. Eventually, I knew we'd have to speak. I mean, we're married, and I couldn't avoid him forever.

"Well, I gotta get ready for class. Hit me later and let me know what you got goin' on tonight. Maybe we can link up after class," I told Brittany.

"Okay! Have a great day!" she said.

I proceeded to get dressed, brush my teeth, and drive

to campus for what would be a long day in class.

As I sat in the quiet, cold classroom, I continued to check the clock. Time went by so slowly, yet I seemingly enjoyed the professor's recent lecture about new technology and machinery. What may be boring to some was totally intriguing to me, and I couldn't wait to dive into my profession. Only a few more semesters, and I would have my degree.

"Keep pushing, Jaz," I whispered to myself as my professor wrapped up his lesson.

Moments after my Tuesday evening class ended, I received a text from Brittany.

Sissy, I'm going to dinner and a movie with some girlfriends. Just givin' you a heads up. I'll be home later tonight. Let's grab dinner together tomorrow, just us, k? Love you!

Knowing I would have the condo to myself, I decided to order takeout and watch a movie, solo dolo. It was the perfect night to stay inside. The sky was black, and a downpour was inevitable. In the past, I would've dreaded a rainy night alone, but I was actually happy about my newfound solo time.

After bearing the dreaded commute from campus, I parked my car in the adjacent parking garage, walked into our apartment building, and took the elevator to Brit's condo on the third floor. Fumbling with the lock, I finally set foot inside, set my keys on the kitchen counter, and stripped down to my t-shirt and panties. Total relaxation. I ordered delivery from a nearby Chinese spot, instructing the delivery person to leave my food at the door. I wasn't about to put pants on, so he would have to drop the food off and dip. Thirty minutes later, I heard a buzzing sound. The delivery man needed access to our building. So, I buzzed him up and he left the food at my front door. I got up from the couch and cracked open the front door, making sure the delivery man was nowhere in sight. I grabbed my food and sat back on the couch.

"Damn," I murmured as I looked out the window. "I should've tipped him more. The rain is really coming down." And it really was. The rain was falling so hard that it looked like a sheet of beads falling from the sky.

Before digging into my fried rice and orange chicken, I heard another buzzing noise. Hopping up from the couch to answer the intercom, I realized the delivery man must have forgotten part of my order.

"Yes?" I questioned, making sure it was the delivery man.

"Jaz, it's me, Cam. You won't answer my messages, and I need to talk to you. I didn't know what else to do so I came by your sister's spot. Please, can we talk?" Cam pleaded. I could barely hear him because the rain was pouring down so hard.

"Cam, go the fuck home. If I didn't answer your calls,

what makes you think I'm going to let you upstairs. Go home," I coldly replied.

"Jaz, please. It's raining hard as shit. Can I have just five minutes?" he begged.

"Nigga, go home! The fuck don't you understand?" I shouted into the intercom, then turning to look at my food, hoping it wasn't too cold at this point.

There was a slight pause, and for a moment I thought Cam had taken my advice and gone home. Suddenly, I heard buzzing noise after buzzing noise. Cam was banging on the buzzer, trying to get my attention.

"Jasmine, I'm pressin' every gotdamn buzzer in this building. I'll wake up this whole fuckin building. I don't give a fuck right now! Give me five minutes, please!" Cam pleaded as he continued to press the other tenants' buzzers, demanding to be let in the building.

Panicked, not wanting him to wake up everyone in the building, especially my neighbors who had twin newborns, I shouted into the intercom, "Damn, Cam, stop fuckin' doing that shit. Fine. You got five minutes. You can talk to me from my front door. You ain't comin' inside, you understand?"

The second I granted him access inside the building, he bolted up three flights of stairs, bypassing the elevator, and knocked at my front door. Knowing damn well he was waiting at the door, I took my time anyway. His ass could wait, I didn't care how frantic he appeared to be.

As I opened the door, I noticed Cam standing there, soakin' wet with his head hung low.

"Jaz," he said as he saw me standing in front of the door, slightly lifting his head to speak. "I... I...," he stuttered as his eyes grew noticeably bigger as he looked at me as I leaned against the wall in my t-shirt and panties.

"You what, nigga?" I asked coldly, unphased by his wet clothes, stutter, and pitiful stance.

Cam stayed silent, and I noticed his shoulders started to slightly shake.

Cam was crying!

That was the first time I ever saw this man cry. He didn't cry when his cousin was unexpectedly shot and killed. He didn't cry when his first label dropped him. He didn't cry when we broke up before, either, but this man was standing at my door, visibly upset, and I believed his devastation.

"You can't leave my life," he quietly said. "I need you, Jasmine. I love you. A nigga fucked up, I know. I'm not perfect. I fucked up, and I will spend forever making this up to you. Please, I need you. Shit don't make sense when you aren't with me."

As Cam stood in the doorway, I felt angry and conflicted at the same time, yet as I saw him cry, I was slightly turned on, too. It was nice to see his emotional side, genuine emotions at that. I looked him up and down while he stood there with his head hung low.

"Save those tears for some other bitch," I coldly said as I closed the door in Cam's face.

Closing the door in his face was the hardest thing I've ever done, but this cycle of cheating and getting my attention again felt like hell. I didn't want this to be our new normal.

I looked through the peep hole of our front door, and Cam was sitting against the adjacent wall with his head in his hands.

"I give that nigga five minutes before he dips," I muttered before turning on the television. Within a matter of minutes of cozying up on the couch, I dozed off. All that drama wore me out, and I ended up taking a two-hour nap. I woke up feeling refreshed, and I as I sat up to stretch on the couch, I heard a sniffling noise. Peering through the peep hole once again, I noticed Cam was in the same sitting position he was in two hours ago. With a heavy sigh, I opened the door.

"Cam, go home. You look pitiful," I said.

"Jaz, this is deeper than me apologizing for cheating. I realize I don't even know how to be a decent husband. My dad wasn't shit, he never stuck around long enough to do right by my mom, and I work in this industry where it's like I'm supposed to be fuckin' new bitches every night. I'm not sayin' the shit is right, I'm sayin' I don't know who the fuck I am, and now it's affecting us," Cam said in between sobs. I could tell he was ashamed, but that didn't change the fact that he disrespected our marriage a mere two months after we promised each other forever.

"I want to be a good man for you, Jaz, but I want to be a good man for me, too, and I don't even know where to start," he said, barely able to look me in the eyes as tears continued to fall down his face.

Slowly, I put my finger on his chin, lifting his face to look at me. Cam's eyes met mine, and we sat there in silence, searching one another's face for answers. Without saying a word, keeping his eyes locked on mine, he leaned in for a hug. He put his head on my shoulder, and I felt his body shake as he continued to quietly cry. He must have had these feelings inside for a while, and I realized his insecurities were piled up inside too, one by one, until he finally couldn't hold them in anymore.

"You're going to get pneumonia if you don't get out of your clothes," I finally said. "You can come inside and change before you go home. I have a few things of yours that you can change into," I quietly offered.

Cam opened the front door and walked back to my bedroom. Before approaching my bedroom door, he turned around and finally spoke again.

"Thank you for letting me change, Jaz. Seriously, I appreciate you."

Watching him get emotional and then undress from his wet clothes made my pussy so wet, and I noticed his dick was hard, too. I sat on my bed, wanting him to take my pussy. He stared in my eyes as he sat down next to me. Cam softly reached for my pussy and started to lightly rub it. I took his hand and directed it to the top of my panties. Cam then slid my white, lace thong to my ankles, and he continued to rub my pussy, I slowly spread my legs, waiting for his dick to enter.

"Are you sure?" he asked, waiting for permission to position himself on top of me.

I nodded, pulling Cam closer to me, directing his dick inside of me. As he put his dick inside me, I felt him release a giant breath of air.

"Damn," he exhaled. "I missed this pussy."

He moved in and out of me, never breaking his stare.

"This my pussy," he whispered, as he licked my breasts until my nipples were rock hard.

"It's yours, Daddy," I whispered back, pulled him into me, feeling his rock-hard dick in the pit of my stomach.

"Lay back," he ordered. "I been waiting for this."

Cam stuck his tongue in my pussy and pushed up as deep as he could. As he sucked my lips and moved to my clit, my legs began to shake. He paused, looked at me, and flashed the slightest yet sexiest smile.

"Turn over," he commanded as he flipped me on to my stomach. Within seconds, we fell into rhythm and I slid on his dick as his right leg pounded against me. Suddenly, he pulled his dick out and ate my pussy again, this from the back, as I creamed all over his tongue.

"You taste so fuckin' good," he moaned, and as he moaned, I quickly snapped out of my trance and reminded myself that this nigga couldn't get the upper hand, so I smoothly slid away from his dick, turned on to my knees, and pushed him on the bed, letting his dick fuck my face. He loved it when I gagged, and I took all ten inches like a pro.

"Gotdamn, Jasmine!" he yelled, and as he yelled, I knew he was about to cum.

I devoured his dick, and all he could do was lay there lifeless. Before Cam was about to bust, he lightly pushed me off him, pulled out of my mouth, and busted on my chest. After pulling the last bit of cum from his dick, he fell back on the bed, directly next to me, and we just sat there and stared at the ceiling.

Cam broke the silence when he turned to me and slyly spoke. "Wanna go again, Baby?"

"Yes, Daddy," I said as I climbed on top, seemingly falling right back into our pattern of fighting and fucking.

CHAPTER EIGHT

After three rounds of intense, aggressive make-up sex, Cam and I hopped in the shower together to wash each other off our bodies. The vibe was peaceful, and as the rain continued to pour outside it added to the mellow mood in the room. Cam squeezed shower gel on my loofa and began to lather me up. As he washed my body, he remained quiet yet seemed at peace. He washed my arms, went slowly across my breasts, and moved down to my legs and feet. He was gentle and paused at random to softly kiss my neck and back. I suddenly felt so safe with him, yet I knew this feeling would quickly come to an end the moment we revisited our rocky reality of a marriage on the brink of divorce. I stayed quiet, though, not exactly wanting to discuss Fortune, his history of

DM'ing other women, and his escapades on the road, although all of that was on my mind. As I was deep in my thoughts, Cam suddenly interrupted my train of thought.

"Jaz, are you going to come home with me?" he asked, sounding a bit cautious to enter this conversation.

"I don't know, Cam," I hesitantly said. "In my heart, I know that you love me, but sometimes love isn't enough. I can't take this back to back cheating. I mean, I get it – you're young, you're on the road, and you have women throwing themselves at you, but damn, you married me knowing this would be your life. You need to consider me in this, too."

"I want to be a better man for you. I really do," he assured.

As we finished washing up, we then stepped out of the shower to dry off.

"I'm really not trying to be here when your sister comes home," Cam said as he dried off his back. "I know she hates me, and I don't even blame her. Let's go back to our place, please. I want to talk to you about something important."

I agreed to go back to our place, mainly because I knew my sister would go ape shit if she walked in and saw Cam in her condo. Plus, I wanted to know what he wanted to tell me. I hate suspense, and I can't stand when someone tells you they need to tell you something.

As I finished getting dressed, I placed his wet clothes in a plastic bag and proceeded to leave Brittany's condo, hand in hand with Cam. We hopped in his Range and started driving back to our place. I noticed the passenger seat hadn't been moved. It was positioned the way I always preferred. I figured that was a good sign, small but seemingly significant. As Cam sped down the highway, I put my hand on his dick and started to rub it back and forth. He looked at me and smiled, and his dick grew hard, fast. Thankful for tinted windows, I unbuckled my seatbelt, leaned over, and bit the bottom of his ear as I unzipped his pants with my right hand and rubbed his dick until it was hard.

"Damn, Jaz. You gon' make me crash, Baby," he moaned.

As I took his dick out from his boxers, I moved my mouth from his ear to his lap, slowly starting to lick the head. As my tongue went around and around, I then took his entire dick into my mouth, allowing the tip to touch the back of my throat. It was only a matter of seconds before he busted. Cam always busted fast when I gave him head in the car.

"I'm about to bust, Jaz," he breathed as I swallowed his cum before he exited the highway.

Feeling satisfied that I made him bust a nut for the fourth time in a matter of a few hours, I popped a piece of gum in my mouth and sat back in my seat.

Cam turned to me, taking his eyes off the road for a second and spoke. "Jaz, if you ever gave that to another man, I would go crazy," he said as he slipped his boxers over his dick and zipped up his pants.

"Wait, so is that why you want to stay married, because you don't want anyone else to have me?" I asked angrily.

"No, Babe. Not at all. That's not what I meant. I meant that I love you and only you, and I don't want to give any nigga a chance to take you from me," Camron explained. "It ain't nobody that could ever make me feel like you do, and I ain't talkin' about the head, although you know you that shit feels good as hell."

"Well damn, think about how I feel knowing you've been inside other bitches, raw at that," I said, and as those words left my mouth, I started to wonder if agreeing to drive back to our home was a mistake.

Within a matter of minutes, we pulled into his parking garage. Cam parked his car and we then walked towards the elevator. I noticed I had a missed text and two missed calls, both from Brittany.

Sis, you good? I came home and you weren't here.

Hesitant to reply, I started to text Brittany, admittedly unsure what to say. I felt slightly foolish because she just told me how proud she was that I didn't cave into Cam.

Hey, sissy. I'll explain everything a little later, but I'm going to Cam's to talk to him about stuff. I hope you aren't upset with me.

Five minutes passed before Brittany finally replied.

I'm not mad at you... I just want what's best for you.

I knew Brittany was more pissed than she led on to, but I appreciated that she gave me space to talk with Cam rather than yelling at me about it.

As we stepped inside Cam's house, I felt a bit out of place. It had been three weeks since I set foot in this apartment, and it no longer felt like mine, only his.

"I'm so glad you're back, Babe," Cam said. "This house ain't a home without you in it."

Lost in my thoughts yet again, I ignored what Cam said and turned to him and asked him what he wanted to discuss.

"Oh, yeah!" he said, remembering what he mentioned to me earlier. "Sit down. I wanted to talk to you about something I've been thinking about, something that would really help our marriage," he excitedly said.

Part of me wondered if this nigga was going to suggest some threesomes or an open marriage. Who knows with Cam. Another part of me wondered if he had a logical solution to our problems such as counseling or going to church together. As I sat down on the couch, I leaned back and waited for him to speak. This was about to get good...

CHAPTER NINE

Cam sat directly next to me on the brown leather sofa in the living room. As he inched closer, he gently picked up my hand and looked me in the eyes. I looked at him crazy, wondering what this dramatic buildup was leading to, hoping he didn't have the audacity to suggest an open marriage. I didn't know what the hell he had up his sleeve, and the anticipation was killing me. I'm down for a lot of shit but an open marriage ain't one, so I hoped that suggestion wasn't about to be put on the table.

"Babe," he began, sounding as if he could hardly contain himself. "I know your final semester presentation for school is coming up, and I was thinking..." he said, trailing off for a brief second to gather his thoughts. "I was thinking that after you finish this semester, you could postpone your fall semester, rejoin in the winter, and come on tour with me instead. We would be together 24/7, and I could show you why our marriage deserves another chance. You'd be with me all the time, and you'd never have to wonder what I'm doing," he excitedly said as if his idea was truly groundbreaking.

I paused, pulled my hand from his, and gave him the nastiest look.

"Don't you see how fucked up this suggestion is?" I angrily questioned.

Cam inched back a bit, shocked by my reaction.

"Wait, Jaz, what do you mean? I'm trying to do everything I can to show you I don't want no other bitch and I want you with me all the time. Last night, Lew told me he booked an entire West Coast tour for me. I'm the headliner, no more opening shows for other performers! And with me being on the road for a few months, I figured you would want to come, too."

Relaxing a bit and scaling back my attitude, secretly excited and proud of him about his tour update, I responded. "Cam, I get that, and I appreciate you trying to think of how we can fix our marriage, but the fact that I would need to abandon school for a semester to go with you on tour just to keep an eye on you pisses me the fuck off. I shouldn't have to do all that to trust you or keep this marriage alive."

"Baby, I don't want you to look at this like something you have to do to trust me, because I'm not going to fuck up regardless. I want you to look at this as something we can share together. You know, going to the West Coast together, touring, and all that shit," he explained, and for a moment, I understood his point. He wanted me to come on tour with him and take a break from school, not to derail me from my dream but to seize this rare chance while a tour opportunity was on the table. I mean, who knows if he would continue to have these opportunities. His career was taking off, but the music industry is unpredictable. One minute you're hot, and the next minute, it's someone else's turn.

"Can you give me some time to think about this?" I asked, not exactly sure I wanted to just go along with his plan and jump at his suggestion. He needed to sweat a little, so I figured a few days wouldn't hurt.

"I have a show in Memphis in three days. We can talk about it when I get back. Is that cool?" Cam asked, seeming to understand my need for more time.

"Yeah, Babe. I'll let you know by then," I said, silently wondering if three days would be enough time to make such a big decision.

***

A few days after our talk on the couch, Cam left for Memphis for his show. He was coming back the following morning, but that didn't mean he wouldn't try to fuck everything moving while he was away. Before he left, he swore he wasn't going to party after his show. I wasn't sure I could believe that, but it was out of my control, so I just had to wait and see if he'd be true to his word.

"I'll have to see it to believe it," I had said, rolling my eyes in his face.

"You'll see, Babe. You'll see," he confidently replied.

The evening of his show, Cam had Lew dial me on Facetime so I could watch his performance, and I was glad he did because the crowd's energy was crazy! From start to finish, the fans were loving Cam's show, and they knew his songs word for word, even the songs he recently released. Cam had a legit fan base! The modest-sized venue was completely sold out, and fans had their phones out to record the show and take pictures of Cam killin' the stage. As uptight as I was with Cam being on the road, I felt so proud watching him in his element. He sounded great and looked even better. As the show wrapped up, Cam walked off stage and Lew and I said our goodbyes as we ended our call. I really enjoyed watching his concert, and I realized that going to the West Coast and watching him in person, night after night, would be an amazing experience.

"I guess I'll have to wait and see what this nigga is about to do," I murmured, not holding my breath as to Cam keeping his promise about not partying after his show. That crowd was electric, so it was hard to believe he would want to party until the wee hours of the morning. Determined to not make myself a nervous wreck about Cam, I snuggled up on the couch with my favorite pink velour blanket and turned on The Game Show channel. I was always a sucker for old school television, and I knew I would be happily distracted with these game shows from the early 90s. Classic. With the remote control in my right hand and a glass of red wine in the other, I didn't even realize an hour had passed. Seconds later, Cam called me via Facetime. I waited a moment before answering, not wanting him to think I was waiting by my phone.

"Hey, Babe!" I cheerfully said as I answered the phone. "You killed it tonight!"

"Thanks, Jaz! The crowd was really into it. I had a good ass time out there. Only thing better would be if you were there," he said with a smile.

Cam always knew what to say, and that wasn't always a good thing.

"So..." I said, pausing to figure out if I would ask about his plans. "What are you about to do tonight?"

"What you mean, Jaz? I told you I'm not goin' out. If you want to spend the night with me on the phone, we can do that. We can watch the same movie or whatever the fuck couples do when they have a Facetime date," he playfully laughed.

"Damn, you're serious!" I replied in disbelief. "I thought you'd go out after your show," I exclaimed, feeling

79

elated that Cam kept his word. "A movie sounds good, but first I got something different in mind," I coyly said as I positioned my phone on the living room table, propping it up against two thick fashion magazines.

Cam sat on the king-size bed in his hotel room and got comfortable for the show that was about to take place. He may have been on stage earlier, but it was my turn to perform.

I slowly took off pants, bending over into the camera to slide off my thong so Cam could see my pussy from the back.

"Damn, you got a fat-ass pussy," Cam said, marveling at his view.

Now naked, I positioned myself on the couch, inserting two fingers deep inside my pussy with the other hand rubbing my breasts. I threw my head back, feeling so good as I rubbed deeper. I slowly removed my fingers and started to suck on them as I watched Cam's dick get harder, working one hand up and down his shaft. His eyes were glued to the screen, awaiting my fingers to re-enter my pussy. I dug deeper, this time moving closer to the camera so he could see the juice on my pussy lips.

"I wanna see you cum," I purred, prompting Cam to cum in clear view.

"And I wanna suck on that thick-ass clit," Cam breathed, and I could hear the desire in his voice.

Cam quickly rose to his feet and started beating his dick to the camera so I could see it. He then grabbed a nearby towel to catch his nut, still fixated on the camera. We were miles apart, but the connection was so intense.

"I wish I was there to swallow that," I said, touching the screen as if I was reaching for his dick.

As Cam busted, I sat back on the couch feeling satisfied that our Facetime date was so steamy.

After busting, he set the phone down, walked to the bathroom, and turned on the shower.

"Give me a few minutes, Babe!" he yelled from the bathroom. "I'm about to jump in the shower."

While Cam took a shower, I decided to do the same. I walked to our master bathroom, turned on the water, and waited a moment before the water got hot. As the steam rose to the top, I entered the shower and quickly lathered up my loofa. I then washed my body from head to toe, rinsed, and turned off the water so I could rejoin Cam for our long-distance date. As I sat back down on the couch in the living room, not feeling like putting on clothes quite yet, I noticed that Cam seemed to have finished up at the same time, too.

"So, you tryna watch a comedy or action movie?" he asked, riffling through his hotel movie selection.

I smiled before answering, admittedly taken aback by Cam's commitment to his word. I mean, I don't know many artists that wouldn't go to the club after their show. Lew had mentioned that Cam backed out of his after-party commitment at a club was that was steps away from his venue, so it definitely seemed like he was trying to win back my trust, but I never really knew with him. Cam was the type to say one thing and do another, even if his heart was in the right place. However, he had never gone to these lengths before to prove I could trust him, and part of me wanted to believe he would stop cheating. The other part of me questioned my sanity, wondering whether Cam could be faithful forever, let alone long stretches of time. Nevertheless, I knew I had two choices – give this marriage another shot and be all in or walk away and never look back. There was no in between, and I wasn't ready to choose the latter.

"Action movie!" I enthusiastically replied, and we both set our phones up so that we could see one another while watching the movie.

"I love you, Jaz," Cam said, smiling into the camera. "I'm glad we're doing this."

"Me too, Cam. Me too," I said, returning a smile.

CHAPTER TEN

When Cam returned from his show in Memphis, he set his bags down and immediately asked me what I decided to do regarding his proposition of joining him on tour.

"Jaz, what's up with L.A.? Did you decide what you're going to do?" he anxiously asked, barely waiting a few minutes upon returning home before bringing up this topic.

"Well, I talked to the admin at my school, and I was able to get permission to take a temporary leave of absence, knowing I'd rejoin the following semester," I replied as I watched Cam erupt in happiness. "I definitely want to be with you when you go on tour, and not so I can keep an eye on you but because I really think this is going to be good for our marriage."

Cam gave me a giant bear-hug, thrilled by my response. As he stepped back, he gave me the most passionate kiss, wrapping his tongue on to mine while pulling me closer. My pussy started to get wet, and I rubbed my hand against his dick. I laughed to myself, thinking that Cam and I can't seem to have a normal conversation without it ending in at least one of us getting turned on. Cam paused for a moment, looked me in the eyes, and smiled.

"This is bout to be lit, Babe!" he excitedly said, taking his phone out to dial Lew to let him know I would be joining Cam on tour.

"The tour starts next week, so we gotta catch a flight in a few days and get there early for sound check and stuff," he said. "Plus, I figure you'll want to get adjusted to the time difference and enjoy some time on the beach, too. I'm tryna see you in that thong," Cam said, laughing at his own joke.

My mind started racing as I thought about packing, cleaning the house, and making sure everything was situated before we left. Traveling for a few months meant leaving our apartment, so I wanted to make sure I had my ducks in a row before we left for the airport. More importantly, I wanted to let my sister know I would be away for a little while. I wasn't sure how she would react, but I was hoping for the best. I never wanted to disappoint her, but something told me she would be happy that Cam and I were going to such great lengths to really make this marriage work, especially as he seemed to put his childish ways behind him.

"Babe, I'm about to run next door and grab us some sushi. I'll be home in 20," he said as he took his wallet and housekeys and left to grab us some lunch.

Cam's quick exit was the perfect time to dial Brittany. Part of me wanted to text her, but I knew this conversation was worthy of a phone conversation. Feeling anxious, I dialed her number and waited for her to answer. By the second ring, Brittany answered the phone, sounded super upbeat. "Hey, sis! What's going on?" she asked, seemingly with her mouth full of food.

"Girl, you know I can't stand when you chew into the phone," I laughed. "I actually wanted to talk to you about something..." I said with apprehension.

"Oh, no. Please don't tell me that Cam is acting a gotdamn fool again. Jaz, I'll go the fuck off, I swear I will," she said as she became irate at the thought.

"No, no! Everything is fine, I swear! In fact, everything is really good. He's growing up and really prioritizing our marriage. I think he's for real this time, too," I said, awaiting her response.

I was met with silence on the other end, unsure if Brittany was waiting for me to continue or if she was rolling her eyes on the other end.

"So," I continued, "he was thinking that I could join him on his West Coast tour. It'll last about three months, and

I already got permission from my professors to take a temporary leave of absence from school. Really, I wanted to call and get your blessing," I said, hoping she would put her feelings for Cam aside and encourage this trip.

I heard Brittany release a heavy sigh on the other end. Then, she began to speak. "Jaz, I just want you to be happy. If you think this trip will help your marriage, I support you, you know that, girl. Now let me find out that nigga is actin' a fool out there, and I'll be on the next flight to wherever the fuck y'all at," she laughed. "But seriously, I'm happy for y'all. I love that he wants you there, and I think this will be good for you guys, too. Make sure to send me lots of videos and pictures, okay?"

I agreed, and we started talking about random shit in each other's lives, from work to school to unimportant gossip. A few minutes later, Cam returned home with our sushi.

"Okay, girl. I'm about to go. Cam just walked in with our lunch. I love you!" I said, feeling elated she supported my decision to go on tour with Cam.

"I love you, too, sis. I'll hit you up later," Brittany said, then hanging up the phone.

As Cam set our sushi on the kitchen counter, he turned to me and asked about my phone conversation with Brittany. "I'm assuming you told Brittany about going on tour. How did that go?" Cam nervously asked. Seeing him squirm about Brittany's response actually made me happy because I could tell he cared about what she thought.

"Actually, she was happy for us. She thinks it'll be good for our marriage," I told Cam.

Cam smiled, relieved by Brittany's reaction to my news.

As we stood in the kitchen and ate our sushi, clearly feeling too greedy to set our lunch up on the dining room table, we ate in silence and enjoyed the fresh rolls from our favorite bistro next door.

"Damn, Cam," I laughed. "How about you come up for air over there," I joked as he shoveled sushi into his mouth.

I finished my salmon roll, cleaned up, and began making a list of what we needed to pack. I needed some sort of order as I prepared us for the road. I realized that attaining order made me feel somewhat in control over my chaotic life, but maybe this was the start of something peaceful, something I no longer had to worry about or try to control. I knew I'd soon find out, one way or another.

CHAPTER ELEVEN

The weeks leading up to our West Coast departure flew by. Between packing, cleaning, and making sure everything was completely squared away with my classroom affairs, we were finally in the air, heading to Cam's first West Coast tour. I tried to play it cool, but inside I was jumping out of my skin. Not only was I about to watch all my man's shows, front and center, but our marriage felt like it was given a second chance, this time with a clean slate and two people who were willing to do anything to make it right. I was no longer the only willing participant in this union, and it felt good to receive the love, attention, and respect I not only deserved but gave him, too. Slowly but surely, my trust issues were disappearing and were replaced with peace. I constantly told myself to just take everything day by day, because with a man like Cam, that's all anyone could really do. He's unpredictable, and to avoid setting myself up for disappointment, I tried to be present in the moment and focus on the now rather than the future. So far, that plan seemed to work, and my nerves thanked me for it.

Although Cam's career was blowing up, he wasn't quite at private-jet status. So, we boarded our commercial flight and enjoyed the perks of first-class seating.

"Guess we can kiss them budget flights goodbye, huh?" Cam joked as he adjusted his seat.

Four hours after our departure, our plane made a smooth land in L.A. Thankfully, our flight was relaxing without any turbulence, and Cam and I both slept for most of the trip. Lew arranged for a car service to pick us up from the airport and take us to our hotel. Lew arrived in L.A. a few days prior to our arrival, just to ensure our hotel and accommodations were up to par.

Cam's West Coast tour kicked off with a fairly long stint in L.A., about three weeks, and he was scheduled to perform at various venues and clubs. Then, we were headed to Arizona for the next leg of his tour. During our first week in L.A., Cam had three shows. Needless to say, it was a busy first week for him, and I could tell he was really excited. His career was taking off, and his songs were being played on every major radio station across the United States. So, this tour was a big deal because it officially marked his status as a rapper on the rise. The man who used to sleep on his grandma's couch and pass out his mixtapes at local clubs was now being stopped in the street for autographs and selfies.

After each performance, Lew booked after-party commitments for Cam, meaning he would have to show up at whichever club Lew had booked him at, party with the guests, and have some drinks. He assured me I would be by his side at every event, so my normal fears and skepticism about the club were now replaced with excitement. I was down to have a good time with my man, especially in the club. Thankfully, I packed accordingly, so I was hype to finally wear a few outfits I had in my closet for a time like this.

"Babe, I'm headed to the beach for a few hours," I said as I grabbed a large hotel towel and scooped my Chanel sunnies from my purse. "By the time you get back from sound check, I'll be back in the room so I can get ready for your show tonight."

This was a new feeling for me – leaving to go somewhere and not worrying about what Cam was doing while we were apart. I couldn't wait to enjoy sun and sand, and what was even better was that the beach was steps from our hotel room.

"Have fun, Jaz!" Cam shouted from the bathroom. "I'll see you in a few hours!"

As I exited the hotel and walked toward the beach, I

looked around and took a moment to thank God. I thanked Him for the positive turn in my marriage with Cam, and I even thanked Him for the hard times that Cam and I experienced because without the hard times, Cam and I would not have grown to a place of peace. I had my man, I had the sand beneath my toes, and I had the sun on my face. Life was good.

***

I glossed over my lips with a thin swipe of tinted lip shine, glanced in the mirror, and slightly adjusted my cleavage. This may have been Cam's first show in L.A., but I was the one who looked like a fucking star. My skin-tight black latex mini dress paired with my patent "So Kate" Louboutin pumps made for one helluva concert outfit. Every curve was accentuated in this dress, and I looked like a walking Coke bottle. I knew what I was doing, too. I'd be damned if my man looked out in the crowd and spotted a badder bitch. Ain't no way.

"Gotdamn, Jaz," Cam said as he walked up on me, smiling and staring at me from head to toe. "You tryna make my dick hard before I get on stage?"

"You tryna give me that dick before we go?" I teased, knowing we had to be in the lobby within the next couple of minutes.

"Oh, you gonna get this dick after the show, believe

that," he said as he joined his hand with mine to head toward the lobby.

I decided to ride with Cam to the venue, even though he had to be there a few hours early. I didn't mind, though. I loved watching the stage crew at work, seeing the crowd pour in, and being able to hang out with Cam before his performance. The plan was to be together throughout the next three months, so I wanted to take advantage of every moment. I viewed these instances as opportunities to really support him and be present during one of the biggest moments in his career, at least one of the biggest moments thus far.

When we arrived at the arena, I slightly nudged Cam. "Can you believe this shit? This is a dream, your dream!" I exclaimed.

"This don't even feel real," Cam said, marveling at the size of the venue. "I'm going to do sound check, so I'll see you later backstage."

He gave me a quick peck on the cheek before walking toward the stage, and I proceeded to make my way toward his dressing room.

Before approaching Cam's dressing room, I spotted Lew who was standing outside of Cam's dressing room door.

"Lew!" I happily shouted. "It's so good to finally see you!" I said as I gave him a big hug.

"Jaz!" he exclaimed, hugging me back. "I'm so happy you could join Cam for his tour. If I had to hold that gotdamn iPhone again for another show, my arm may fall off," he joked. "But seriously, Cam is so happy you agreed to come, and I'm happy to see you, too. Hopefully, my wife and kids can join us in Arizona. Well, join us there but not go to the show of course," he laughed, knowing the language of Cam's songs wasn't exactly suitable for his three-year-old and five-year-old daughters.

I couldn't help but chuckle to myself because Lew stood out like a sore thumb at the venue. Hell, he stood out among all of his Cam's shows. Lew stood tall at six feet, five inches, and his bright red hair could be noticed from a mile away. His pale skin and freckles added to the anomaly of his presence at a hip hop show. Nevertheless, he was like family, and it felt great to see a familiar face while I was so far from home.

"I'm going to take my seat," I told Lew. "I'll catch you backstage after the show!"

We exchanged one last hug, and I walked toward the front row of the venue, positioning myself at the center of the stage. Cam told me I could sit wherever I wanted, whether that was in the front row or behind stage. This time, I wanted to enjoy the concert vibe as any concert goer, so I chose front row to get the entire experience.

As I glanced at the time on my phone, I realized Cam's show was about to start in the next 30 minutes. People were arriving early, packing in the venue one by one. Lew had said this would be a sold-out show, so I was looking forward to

Cam walking on stage to see a massive crowd. There was something peaceful about people-watching, so I hardly minded waiting for the show to start. The crowd was so eclectic. From teenage white chicks to frat boys to an urban crowd in their late 20s and early 30s, Cam's music clearly attracted all types of people. That's the point of music though – to unite people and have a good time.

Before I knew it, the lights were dimmed, and the crowd erupted into applause and screaming. Most people held up their phones to film Cam's entrance. The arena place was live! Cam walked out on stage and started rapping the words to his recent hit, "Who Me?" I rapped along with Cam and the crowd, wishing my sister was next to me to enjoy this dope ass show. She may have hated Cam, but she loved his music. As the show wrapped up, I caught Cam's eye and he gave me a sly grin. I was so turned on by his performance, and as weird as this may have seemed, I was turned on by everyone screaming for him, too.

As the crowd started to file out of the venue, I made my way backstage to meet Cam. Much to my surprise, there wasn't a flock of groupies waiting for him by his dressing room. There were some chicks with backstage passes, but they seemed to be women who purchased the meet-and-greet package. I didn't mind if they met Cam, as long as their "greet" didn't mean trying to fuck him. Lew had let me into Cam's dressing room, but Cam was in the shower. After his performance, he was probably a sweaty mess.

"Hey, Baby! You killed it tonight!" I said as I peeked into the shower. "I'm going to wait on the couch, okay? I don't want to fuck up my makeup before we go to the club," I told him as I backed away from the steam rising from his shower.

"Thanks, Jaz! The place was packed, right?! This shit feels surreal! I'm really glad you're here, Baby. Give me a second to dry off and get dressed. I'll see you in a few minutes," Cam said, turning toward the water to finish rinsing off.

Cam hurriedly dried off and put on a new outfit, a pair of distressed denim, red bottom sneakers, and a fitted white t-shirt. He threw on his new diamond chain and diamond-studded Rolex and made his way to the fans who were waiting for a picture and autograph. In a matter of 15 minutes, Cam had signed 50 autographs and took pictures with everyone waiting backstage. Lew moved the line along quickly, thank God.

"Thanks for waiting," Cam said as he pulled me in for a kiss. "You ready for the club?" he asked, grabbing my hand and guiding us toward the exit.

"Hell yeah!" I replied, happy as hell to be able to party with my man. My school schedule hadn't really allowed for much down time, so this was the first time in a long time that I was about to turn the fuck up and have a good time. Our car service awaited, and off we went to the club.

They say never to bring sand to the beach, but Cam knew damn well I'd drown his ass if he broke my trust at this point, especially with how great things have been. I figured we'd soon find out if going to the club together was a good idea.

CHAPTER TWELVE

Our table was already set up for us when we arrived, and we were positioned on the center stage by the DJ. L.A. clubs were off the chain, two and three stories high, and the bottle girls looked more like high fashion models than regular waitresses. A busty redbone with long braids came over to ask us if we needed anything. We both declined, as our table was already stocked with white and dark liquor, a ton of chasers, and some random trays of food. Cam already knew my drink of choice was dark, so he poured me a shot and I quickly tossed it back. Dark liquor makes some people angry. For me, dark liquor brought out my wild side, and I was tryna turn up.

Within a few minutes of settling into our booth, the DJ introduced Cam, and the crowd went crazy. L.A. was showing him so much love, and I could tell he was enjoying every second of it. I couldn't even blame him. He worked hard for these moments, and I loved that I could see him shine. As we peered over the balcony, vibin' to the music, I saw a few chicks eyein' Cam and trying to make their way to our table. He saw their thirsty asses, too. I mean, their eyes were glued to him, and it was obvious they wanted him to notice them. Our table was huge but there were only four of us at the time – me, Cam, and his boys that worked as part of the stage crew – so I had a hard time believing they were eyeing Cam's friends. I knew they wanted Cam, and I guess this was something I needed to get used to. This part of being on tour was exactly what I was dreading – dealing with the groupies and constant attention. I let out a big sigh, stepped away from the balcony, and tossed back another shot. Cam must have noticed the change in my energy because he grabbed me by the waist and softly kissed my neck.

"I'm here with you, Babe. Fuck them hoes," he said over the loud ass music.

I smiled, refilled my shot glass, and threw back my third shot in a matter of 30 minutes. I wanted to have a good time, and I also didn't want to spend my night worrying about the women in this club. None of these hoes had shit on me, but I felt awkward in knowing that my man had the attention of every chick in the building. Being on tour with Cam was great, but the groupie aspect was the worst. Quickly becoming lost in my thoughts, I started to question if I could deal with this, night and night out, and I wondered whether Cam would be able to resist these women every night. Suddenly, the beat dropped to one of my favorite songs, thankfully interrupting the toxic conversation I was having in my mind, and I started twerking on the table.

"Ayeeee!" Cam shouted, laughing at my random turn up.

As I looked up, I noticed everyone on the lower level staring at us and cheering me on. The liquor in me started to talk, so I slightly pulled up my latex dress, which was damn near glued to my body, and I shook my ass to the beat. I couldn't remember the last time I had this much fun! As I was dancing, Cam got behind me and put his hands on my ass. Ain't no way he was about to have me shake my ass up here and not let people know I was his. Just as thirsty as the women were in L.A., so were the men, and he knew it. As I shook my ass on him, he slowly slid his fingers up my dress and subtly moved my thong to the side. I looked back at Cam, and he smiled. That nigga was always down to do some freak shit in public, and he knew I loved every second of it. Having someone watch you or wonder what the fuck is going on was a total turn on. I motioned for him to sit on the couch so he could really feel on me. Now bouncing on his lap with his fingers going in and out of me, I felt my pussy warm up. No longer giving a shit about who was watching, I pulled my dress up a little more, now with the bottom of my ass peeking out, and I let Cam finger-fuck me until my pussy felt like it would explode. One of Cam's boys poured him a shot and Cam tossed it back with his other hand while I came all over his fingers. With the music still blaring and his boys watching us like we were a live porno, I got down on my knees, pulled Cam's hand to my mouth, and sucked my cum off his fingers.

He sat there, dick hard as a rock, and stared at me wide eyed. "These people got two shows tonight," Cam said in my ear as he pulled my face close to his.

"You ready to leave?" I asked, suddenly wanting to leave the club and just be with my man.

"You not having a good time?" Cam asked, seemingly concerned about my sudden change in mood.

"I'm havin' a great time!" I assured him. "I just want the dick, and I don't think I want to wait another two hours to get it," I said, flashing Cam a devious grin.

Cam's eyes grew as big as quarters, and I knew he wanted to leave the club just as bad as I did. He looked at his phone to check the time and told his boys to call our car service. We stayed as long as we needed, according to his contract, so we were free to go and enjoy the night the way we wanted to enjoy it which meant a night of suckin' and fuckin'.

"Let's go," Cam said, taking one more shot before standing up. "I'm tryna get you out that dress... but you better keep them heels on," he said as he grabbed my hand and led us out the club.

Our driver was already waiting out front in a black, four-door Mercedes. Like a true gentleman, Cam opened the right-side passenger door for me and helped me in. Then, he went around to the other side and got in the vehicle. As we drove off, random people were trying to wave him down and get his attention, but there was no way we were about to stop. We could barely keep our hands off each other in the car, and although the hotel was a few blocks away, it felt like miles. The fire Cam and I had between us felt as if it was our first time every time, and that electric connection was something I hoped we would always share. One of my girlfriends once told me that you can't have good love without good sex, and I was starting to see her point.

Our first night in L.A. was everything I thought it would be and more – flashy, exciting, entertaining, and wild. I mean, we were right near Hollywood, so some drama was to be expected.

As we pulled into our hotel and the driver inched us as close as he could to the hotel's entrance, I realized that my buzz started to wear off and I regretted not taking another drink before leaving the club. I hoped the hotel manager put a few bottles of champagne on ice in our room. Suddenly, a million thoughts swirled through my mind, and I started to wonder if every night would be this good or if things were too good to be true between me and Cam.

CHAPTER THIRTEEN

When Cam and I arrived at our hotel suite after his club appearance, we drank both bottles of champagne that the hotel manager had left for us, and we ended up staying awake until 7 am. The liquor made Cam last all night, and I wasn't mad at it. Thankfully, he didn't have a show the following day, so we were able to sleep in and enjoy a good night's sleep. Around noon, Cam rolled over to my side of the bed and gave me a kiss on the forehead.

Groggy but happy, I opened my eyes to face my man. "I could get used to this," I smiled and said as I noticed we slept in later than we had in a long time. The clock read noon, and I couldn't believe we didn't wake up to the sound of our phones, both of which we forgot to put on silent.

"Good," Cam said, "because we have two months and 29 days left, so I hope you enjoy every minute of this," Cam happily said. "Let's have lunch on the beach. Lew said there's a nearby taco spot that's fire."

Agreeing with Cam's plans to venture out for lunch, especially because tacos were involved, I lazily got out of bed and hopped in the shower. I knew I must have been drunk last night because I went to sleep with my makeup on, and I never do that. No matter how much I drink, I always manage to find my way to the bathroom to wash my face. However, the shots and countless glasses of champagne eliminated any chance of following through with my pre-sleep routine.

A few moments later, Cam entered the shower to join me, and we enjoyed our usual shower routine together as we washed one another from head to toe. Deep down, I loved hogging the shower and making the water piping hot, unlike Cam who preferred lukewarm water. I would never tell him that, though. Nevertheless, I loved having him close.

After we washed and rinsed our bodies, I turned off the water, and we both stepped out of the shower to dry off and get ready for lunch. If I had been home in Atlanta, I would've been on campus, walking to my second class of the day, yet I was in L.A., living for the moment and enjoying a random lunch with my man by my side. Taking a short break from my school responsibilities didn't feel as bad as I thought it would. In fact, I was enjoying this rare downtime. As much as I loved school, and as close as I was to earning my degree, I also enjoyed this spur-of-the-moment travel time with Cam. I hate to admit this, but he was right – this was a once-in-a-lifetime experience, and I had yet to regret dropping everything and leaving on a jet plane with my man.

As Cam secured his watch around his wrist and I double checked my purse to make sure I had my sunglasses, Cam's phone began to ring.

"My nigga!" Cam happily shouted into the phone, erupting into laughter. "The fuck you up to, my G? Where you at?"

I had a gut feeling Cam was talking to his best friend, Mike. Mike was Cam's childhood best friend, and Mike had recently moved to San Diego. I knew it was only a matter of time until Mike reached out to Cam regarding Cam's West Coast tour. I didn't have a problem with Mike, so to speak, but he was that friend Cam always got into trouble with. Staying out 'til 7 am, being around a bunch of bitches, and spending too much money, that was Cam and Mike. Now that I think about it, I didn't really like Mike; I tolerated him because that was Cam's boy, but if I had my way, they wouldn't have a friendship. The dude was trouble, and to make matters worse, he was single. In fact, he was perpetually single. You could basically say he was allergic to commitment. I've known Mike for years, and I've never known him to have a serious girlfriend. He had girls, but never a girlfriend. He was that type of dude. My mama always told me that a married man shouldn't have too many single friends, if any at all, and I always kept that piece of advice in the back of my mind.

"Yea, my nigga! Come through! I'll have Lew get you a room at our hotel, and you can roll to the next show with Jaz!" Cam said, and I immediately rolled my eyes, already dreading Mike's arrival, whenever that would be.

A few minutes later, Cam hung up the phone, and I could tell he was beyond happy about his friend coming to town. It had been a few years since they had last seen each other, so I knew Cam wanted to turn up with Mike. Selfishly, I didn't want Mike to intrude on our time together, especially because everything started off so great. Nevertheless, I decided to keep my thoughts to myself, grin, and bear it for the day or two Mike stops through L.A.

"Babe!" Cam exclaimed. "Mike is comin' to my next show! He'll be here tomorrow, and he's going to stay for a day or two."

A day or two...

Knowing Mike, one day would turn to two which would turn to ten. Despite my irritation, I turned to Cam and smiled. "Aw, Babe! I'm so happy for you! You haven't seen Mike in a minute, huh?" I said, pretending to be excited over this less than stellar news.

"I got my wife here, and my best friend about to be here! This bout to be lit!" Cam said as he grabbed my hand

and escorted us out of the hotel.

Mike was supposed to arrive in L.A. a few hours before Cam's show. So, I told myself to be ready so we could go to the show together. Deep down, I knew I needed to prepare for much more than Mike's arrival.

***

The following day, the day of Cam's second show, Mike and I met outside the arena so I could show him to our seats.

"Hey, Sis!" Mike said as he greeted me before walking into the venue.

"What's up, Mike?" I said, trying my best to give him a warm greeting. We made our way to our seats and had small talk before Cam's show began.

All two hours and 15 minutes of Cam's show was lit, and I was impressed that he kept the same energy as his last show. Being on stage for a long performance seems exhausting, especially when you rap the same songs over and over, but he was hype as if this was his first and only show. The crowd was really into him, and Mike was actually pretty cool throughout the show. He vibed to the music and we had a few drinks during the show. All in all, he didn't drive me crazy or bring any sleezy chicks around, either. As the show came to an end, and Cam performed his last song, Mike and I made our way backstage to meet Cam. As we approached Cam's dressing room, several women were waiting at the nearby meet-and-greet table.

"I'll be right back," Mike said to me as his eyes were fixated on the women near Cam's table. "I'm tryna holla at ol' girl in the leather pants," Mike said, licking his lips like a total creep.

Before I could reply, Mike was already making his way to table of girls, and as I gave the group of women a closer look, I noticed two women who seemed a bit familiar. I couldn't put my finger on it, but I knew them from somewhere.

"Oh, shit!" I said aloud, not realizing I was basically talking to myself. It suddenly dawned on me who those chicks were that stood by Cam's meet-and-greet table. I whipped out my phone and slyly took a picture to send Brittany.

Within seconds, Brittany replied to my picture text.

What the hell is bum-ass Mike doing near those cute women? They don't want his ass LOL!

Although I didn't know the woman Mike was trying to approach, I recognized her two friends, one of which was dating a well-known female boxing champ. I chuckled to myself, waiting for Mike to hit on her, knowing she wasn't into dick. Her friend, though, was a known industry bitch, and everyone knew she was always waiting for the next big thing to buy her a bag or some shoes, and all she had to do was suck a dick for something designer and gas him up on Instagram.

Typical IG thot shit. Nevertheless, I text my sister back before Mike headed back my way.

Girl, yes! That's her! She must've been here for the show, but I have my eye on her hoe-ass friend. I already know what kind of game she tries to pull at these shows. I'll text you later though. Love you!

As I placed my phone back into my clutch, Mike started to walk back my way.

"You get her number?" I asked Mike, pretending to actually give a damn whether they exchanged numbers.

"Of course," he arrogantly replied. "She about to meet me at the club after this," he smiled, and as he looked at her number in his phone, my blood started to boil. I silently hoped Cam wouldn't be on some fuck shit tonight just because Mike wanted to be his usual scheming self.

A few minutes later, Cam came out of his dressing room.

"Hey, Baby!" Cam said as he gave me a kiss on the cheek, then dapping up Mike.

"You killed that show!" I said as I rubbed on his chest.

I knew the chicks from his meet-and-greet table were looking my way, so I wanted to make sure they knew what was up... even though those sorts of chicks couldn't careless whether Cam was married.

"Thank you, Babe. I'm about to handle this meet-and-greet, and I'll meet y'all back at the hotel so we can go to the club," Cam said, giving me another kiss before Mike and I left for the hotel.

I wanted to stay for the meet-and-greet, but I didn't want him to realize I was hanging around to keep an eye on him. Things have been good with us, so I didn't want to mess that up. So, Mike and I proceeded to call an Uber back to the hotel and wait for Cam. Determined not to let this change my energy, I pushed it out of my mind and figured I would see Cam shortly for what's sure to be a fun, wild ass night at the club.

***

One hour later, Cam walked into our hotel suite.

"Let's go!" he excitedly said, looking a little bit buzzed as he motioned for us to leave with him for the club.

"Damn, Babe. You already started gettin' it in, huh?" I asked jokingly but half serious.

"Chill, Babe. Chill. I'm just tryna turn up before we get to the club. I gotta show Mike a good time tonight! I ain't seen my nigga in a minute," Cam loudly said, walking over to Mike to give him five.

As Mike and Cam stood in the opposite corner of the suite's living room, I saw Mike pull out his phone to show something, assumedly that girl's number from the meet-and-greet. The two started speaking more quietly until I walked over to break up their little pow wow.

"Jaz, you don't mind if I take Mike to the club tonight, do you? We ain't went out together in a minute, so I'm tryna show him what L.A. is all about," Cam said as he nuzzled my ear, clearly trying to butter me up so they could go to the club alone.

I paused for a moment and my body tightened up. The last thing I wanted was for Cam to go to the club without me. He must have sensed my apprehension because he quickly spoke up.

"You can trust me, Baby. Imma show up for my club appearance, pop some bottles with my dawg, and come home to you. Is that cool?"

"Yeah... I guess that's okay. I thought I'd go with you tonight, but I guess we have the next three months to party together," I reluctantly said.

"You're the best," Cam said, pulling me in for a kiss. "I'll see you later, okay?"

The guys left our suite, and I immediately undressed and put on an oversized white robe from the hotel bathroom. As I flopped on the king-size bed, I grabbed the remote control and started browsing the movies.

"I'll rent a movie and order room service," I said aloud, determined to stay distracted until Cam came back. I didn't want my mind to wander, and I didn't want to start digging around his Instagram, either. I figured what's done in the dark comes to light, anyway. Two romantic comedies and a plate of $25 chicken fingers later, Cam came strolling in our hotel suite, clearly drunk from his night at the club. He was stumbling as he made his way toward the bed, and he tripped over his own foot as he approached my side of the bed.

"Heyyyy, Jath," Cam slurred, leaning down to give me a kiss.

Watching someone drunk off their ass while you're sober was annoying as fuck, and tonight was no exception.

"You look like you had a good time," I managed to say, clearly irritated by his antics.

"Take off that robe," Cam said, aggressively rubbing his hands on my breasts. "You been waiting for daddy, huh?"

"Boy, you so stupid," I laughed as I let Cam slide his hand up my robe, making his way to my pussy. I may have been annoyed, but I was horny as hell, too.

Cam stood back up to unzip his pants, obviously trying his best to keep his balance. He pulled out his dick from his boxers, and it was already hard, just waiting to penetrate me.

I motioned for Cam to sit down as I climbed on top of him and slid my pussy on all ten inches of his hard dick. Cam slammed me into his dick even harder, gripping my waist with each motion. I slowed down and grinded into him, and he placed his hands around my neck, gentle gripping me as my juices saturated him. Even though he was drunk, he knew exactly what I liked. With each movement, Cam groaned louder.

"Gotdamn, Jaz, I'm about to bust."

I quickly glanced over at the clock on my nightstand. It had only been three minutes, and I wasn't about to cum, but Cam looked as though he had no more than 30 seconds left in him. In a matter of a few seconds, he came inside of me, and fell back on to the bed while I remained on top of him.

"Damn, girl," he said under his breath.

Slightly irritated and now wide awake, I climbed off his lap and walked to the bathroom to take a shower. I figured I would play with myself in the shower, because there was no way I could go to sleep while I was this horny. As I was lathering my washcloth with soap, Cam shouted from the bed. "Jaz, you mind if I go to Mike's room really quick? He said he need to talk to me."

Stepping away from the heavy streams of water, I shouted back. "Why can't he just call you?"

"Man, I don't know, Jaz! I'll be right back though," Cam said, and off he went without waiting for my response.

The entire evening felt sketchy, except for Cam's show, and I was beginning to feel uncomfortable. I knew this feeling, and as much as I hated it, my intuition was always right. My gut was warning me that Cam was up to no good. As I rinsed off, I thought about what I would do or say. I didn't want to rock the boat, but I didn't want to be a doormat, either. I also didn't want to bust down Mike's door, just in case nothing was actually going on. That would make me look like a crazy fool. Ultimately, I decided I would talk about it with Cam in the morning. It was already six in the morning, and I wasn't in the mood for anything other than a few hours of rest. Well, that and an orgasm.

CHAPTER FOURTEEN

Cam came back from Mike's room around eight in the morning, a whole two hours after he left our suite. When I heard him come in, I couldn't help but notice the time on the nearby clock. Either Cam was creeping with Mike on the low or he was fuckin' a chick in Mike's room. I ruled out any other option because not only was Cam drunk, but he wasn't the type to stay up at six in the morning to chit chat with his boy. Nevertheless, after noticing the time, I closed my eyes and went back to sleep for another couple of hours. Yesterday's antics were exhausting, and I wasn't exactly ready to have a drawn-out conversation about our marriage. First, I needed more sleep.

Around noon, Mike knocked on our door. "Damn, is

this nigga obsessed with you or what?" I said to Cam as he continued to snore and ignore Mike's persistent knocks. I got up, threw on my robe, and reluctantly answered, knowing he would continue to knock if one of us didn't come to the door.

"What up, Jaz?" Mike cheerfully asked as he made his way into our suite.

"Sure, come on in," I mumbled, ignoring his annoyingly chipper greeting. Instead of having small talk with my least favorite person, I walked to the bathroom to brush my teeth. A few seconds later, Cam walked in the bathroom.

"Hey, Baby! Shit, last night was wild. Mike had a good time. Thanks for being so cool about us going out," Cam said, clearly ignoring the fact that he left the room for a whole two hours after our three-minute quickie. Either he thought I didn't care, or he was trying to smooth things out so I wouldn't mention the fact that he basically ditched me last night.

I rinsed off my toothbrush, wiped the toothpaste from around my mouth, and decided now was a good time to talk to Cam. I would be damned if this shit continued for the remaining time I was on tour with him. So, I figured we could either talk now or Mike would have to hear our conversation when we all step out for lunch, and I certainly didn't want the latter.

"Cam, we gotta talk," I said as I turned my attention to him. I've been trying to hold this in, but I can't anymore. Going to the club without me and then leaving the room 'til 8 am, this shit doesn't feel right, and it's starting to feel too familiar... and that's not a good thing," I said as I stared directly into his eyes, and he knew exactly what I was implying.

"Man, Jaz, don't start trippin'. Look, I took Mike out and I went to his room to chill for a few hours. That's it. I ain't do nothin' forreal. We were just kickin' it."

His response was flippant, not exactly concerned with my feelings, but he wasn't cold or entirely dismissive, either.

"I'm about to run to the gas station really quick and grab some blunts. I'll be back here in 15 minutes," Cam said, abruptly ending our conversation and grabbing his wallet off the bathroom sink.

Mike followed behind Cam like a puppy dog, and off they went to pick up some blunts, or say he said.

Feeling frustrated, wondering when we would resume our conversation, I began walking toward the closet to decide what to wear to lunch. Out of the corner of my eye, I noticed a black cell phone on the hotel desk. The phone nearly blended into the desk, so I almost walked right past it. Cam's phone was gold, so I assumed Mike accidentally left his phone behind before they went to the gas station. I picked up the phone, and the home screen was a picture of Cam performing from his recent show.

"That's weird as hell," I murmured, confused as to why Mike had a picture of my man on his home screen.

Momentarily shrugging off the bizarre photo Mike chose for his home screen, I made my way to his texts.

"Typical," I said aloud as I noticed a rack of texts from a bunch of women labeled as "blonde from the club," "big titties black shirt," and "pink dress."

You comin' to my show tonight, Baby? I got you a ticket. It will be at will call.

Girl, stop playin' with me. I know you about to gimme that pussy when I see you in Arizona.

Make sure you check the mail today. I sent you that bag you had your eye on. Send me a picture of that pussy. I need to see it before you sit on my face again.

"Oh my god…" I whispered.

The phone wasn't Mike's; it was Cam's! Cam had a secret phone he was using, and he was talking to more girls than I could keep count of, including the bitch from last night's show who was supposedly in love with her girlfriend. I guess she liked dick after all.

Daddy, you looked good last night. Thanks for giving us passes to your show. Will I see you again tonight?

"Fraud-ass bitch," I mumbled, wishing I had her girlfriend's number so I could let her know that her woman was on the hunt for some dick. Knowing Cam would be back in a matter of seconds, I saved a few of the numbers in my phone and set the black phone back on the desk in the exactly place I found it. Cam thought he was slick by having a burner phone, but little did he know I was about to turn the tables on his ass. I decided to play it cool, as if I never saw anything. That way, I could buy myself enough time to figure out how I would get the fuck out of L.A. and back to Atlanta, this time as a single woman.

***

Sitting through lunch was torture. I barely touched my salad. I wasn't one to fake my emotions, but I knew no one in L.A., and I didn't want to make a move until I had a first-class ticket back to L.A. and some change in my pocket.

"Jaz, why you so quiet?" Cam asked.

"I'm good!" I said perkily, trying to exercise my best acting skills. "I'm just tired as hell, that's all. I'll take a nap when we get back to the room," I casually said, playing off my quietness for exhaustion.

After Cam paid the bill, the three of us stood up and made our way to the exit.

"Are you about to nap at the hotel?" Cam asked.

Normally, this question would come from a concerned place, but I knew he was asking me because he had plans with Mike that didn't involve me.

"Yeah, I think I'm going to sleep for a little bit before your show," I lied. Really, I just wanted to be alone and away from his ass.

"Cool. I'm about to hit up the mall with Mike and get some shoes. I'll see you a little later," Cam said, giving me a kiss on the cheek as he turned to walk in the opposite direction with Mike.

A few hours later, Cam returned to our room. I was covered in the hotel robe again with a washcloth on my forehead.

"You okay, Babe?" Cam asked as he walked over to me.

"Babe, I feel really sick. I don't know if it was something I ate or what, but I don't think I can go to your show tonight," I lied.

Cam had to fight back his excitement over my news, to which he poorly hid with a concerned frown. "I understand, Jaz. I'll make sure Lew keeps his phone on in case you need anything while I'm performing, okay? I need to get ready to meet Mike in the lobby so we can leave for my show. I'll see you back here after my club appearance, okay?"

I nodded my head and turned my cheek so Cam could give me a quick kiss, definitely taking my I'm-so-sick act to the next level. Not only that, but I didn't want that man's lips anywhere near me. I figured the duration of his show and club appearance would buy me enough time to conjure up a lie about returning home, convince Lew to book me a flight, pack my bags, and head back to Atlanta to start finding a divorce attorney.

Being on the road with Cam wasn't enough to save our

marriage. Facetiming while apart wasn't enough to permanently fix us, either. The only thing that could fix Cam was Cam, and he wasn't ready for all that. He wasn't in a mental and emotional space to endure serious growth, and I wasn't in a space to accept this as the standard for our marriage. He might have thought he was in a space to be the best man he could be, and he might have wanted to give his all, but he ultimately fell short and my heart was growing cold to it all.

Oh, and there was one more part to my plan that I fully intended to execute before leaving L.A. – create a group chat with the phone numbers I saved from Cam's phone, and text the bitches who had no regard for my marriage. Cam would be on stage for the next several hours, so I certainly had time to pull this off without a hitch.

As I heard the elevator door close, I knew Cam was on his way out of the hotel. So, I picked up my phone and started a group chat with me, the pseudo-lesbian, the wannabe Instagram model, and whomever was saved in Cam's phone as "big titties black shirt."

Ladies, or rather, hoe-ass homewreckers, this is Jasmine, Camron's wife. You know, Camron, the man you've all been texting and having side relationships with, despite his marriage to me. I figured I would give you a heads up about his marital status and let you know that you can shoot your best shot without having to sneak around anymore because our marriage is over. Thank you for making this an easy decision for me. If you think he won't cheat on you, think again. Then again, I'm sure some of you only want a bag and some shoes, the usual goals you aspire to achieve. Hopefully, you get tired of being a bum bitch and you find your own bag and a man who isn't married.

Within a matter of minutes, the texts started to pour in, some were blatant lies, some were self-defense, and others were total disregard for my feelings. The first text was from the woman who was said to be dating the popular female boxer.

Cam and I are strictly friends. I have a girlfriend that I love, and he and I are friends and only friends.

I wanted to respond to her and call her out because what "friend" calls her other male friend "daddy," but she wasn't worth my time. I didn't want Cam back, and she could have him, if that's what she wanted, so responding to her text wasn't needed. I found it funny, however, that she would learn through this group text that she and her friend were both vying for Cam's attention. They may have already known, who knows, but at least I could get a laugh out of their stupidity.

The Instagram model's response came as no surprise: *I can't help it if your man wants to buy me gifts. Who am I to turn down free Chanel?*

Typical.

The other woman never answered, and I figured that

suited her identity just fine because she didn't even have a name in Cam's phone.

As I closed out of the group text, I sent Lew a message about needing a flight home.

Hi, Lew! I know Cam is on stage, so I can't talk to him about this right now, but my sister is moving out of her condo and needs my help. I figure I could go back and help her and then come back to L.A. to be with Cam. I only need a few days. She doesn't have anyone there to lend a hand, so I don't want to leave her high and dry. Can you book me a red-eye flight?

I set my phone down, pleased by my convincing lie, and started to gather my belongings from the hotel bathroom. Lew was normally speedy when it came to responding to my texts, so I figure I should have an answer, and hopefully a flight home, within the hour.

As time went on, however, Lew never replied, and I started to panic. Cam's show was scheduled to end soon, and I really wanted to have my flight set in stone before I saw him. I wanted out of this marriage, and I wanted this to be seamless for me, especially considering Cam had already put me through so much hell. A peaceful departure was the least of what I deserved. I had a backup plan, though. If Lew didn't reply, I would text Cam with the same request. He was cheating on me every chance he had, so I doubted he would put up much of a fight if I lied and said I needed a few days to help Brittany move into a new place.

The time had come to text Cam because Lew had not responded. Hopefully, Cam would answer me and arrange my flight before he got too drunk at the club with Mike.

"Hey, Cam! Brit called me earlier and told me she's unexpectedly moving. I know I said I'd stay in L.A. with you, but would you mind if I left for a couple of days, helped her move, and then came back to be with you? I would need to go immediately, because she's trying to pack up by tomorrow."

At this point, my stomach was in knots. I wasn't a good liar, and I just wanted to know that I would home soon without having to fake actually caring about this fool for another minute.

Once midnight rolled around, and Lew and Cam still hadn't replied, I began to get nervous.

"Why hasn't anybody answered me?" I muttered, confused as to why everyone was ghost.

The only thing I could do at that point was wait...

CHAPTER FIFTEEN

Cam strolled into our hotel room around noon the following afternoon, as if he hadn't been out all night and morning. Without saying hello or remotely caring about his disrespectful timing, he sat on the bed, grabbed the remote control, and proceeded to turn on the television. At the very least, I expected a half-ass explanation about where he was, but he didn't so much as say a peep.

As I watched Cam nonchalantly flip through the channels, basically ignoring the fact that we were in the same room together, I bolted from the desk chair, grabbed the remote control from his hands, and threw it against the wall with all my might.

"Nigga, are you fuckin' kidding me right now? You got

the nerve to waltz in here at noon, not speak, and act like you ain't been out all night? You got me all the way fucked up, Cam!" I screamed as I stood over him on the bed, truly not giving a damn about the other people on our floor.

"Man, I ain't tryna hear all that. I'm really not. You either gunna accept the shit or you ain't, because I'm not about to be on my best behavior every second of the fuckin' day. This shit is exhausting," Cam casually replied, dramatically leaning back on a pillow as if he just ran a marathon.

"Being a decent husband is exhausting?" I demanded at the top of my lungs. "You proposed to me, Cam! I didn't make you walk down the aisle, and I didn't make you take me to L.A., either. You begged me! You asked me to come, and now you wanna act like this? I could've stayed my ass in Atlanta!" I screamed, feeling myself losing all control over my emotions. It's one thing to be sad but add anger on top of the sadness and the combination of emotions becomes an outward expression of rage like none other. "I asked you for a flight home and you could've booked me one last night, but you chose to ignore me instead!"

Once the words started to flow, they wouldn't stop. All the pent-up anger, disrespect, and times I bit my tongue and suppressed emotions began to surface, and I knew I could no longer hold back.

"How could you, Cam?! I put my life on hold for you,

nigga! I left school to be with you. I trusted you when you said I should come on tour with you, and this is the shit you do? This is your idea of fixing our marriage?" I screamed as tears poured down my face. Last night, I couldn't wait to get the fuck out of L.A., but that was on my terms. Today, I was angry all over again that everything, yet again, was on Cam's time and according to Cam's plan. It was hard for me to believe that a week ago, we were in the best space of our marriage, and suddenly, shit was going south again. All the love and trust I invested in this man were now wasted emotions, and I felt like a total fool for ever thinking he could be the husband I deserved. He may have shown glimpses of being a good husband, but the only thing he really proved was that he was unable to consistently be the man I deserved and needed. I wasn't willing to accept a part-time husband or a man who could only sometimes commit to loving, faithful behavior. I was all in, and I needed him to be all in, too, but for the first time, I realized I only had myself to blame for expecting Cam to be more than a part-time husband and less than a full-time deceiver. This marriage was over, and I knew in my heart that once I left this room, that would not only be the end of us, but it may be the last time we ever see each other again. There was nothing else to say and nothing we could do to fix this. We were at the end of our rope, and we both knew it. The memories we made in L.A. were seemingly not so special because they were now clouded by our reality, a reality that we were doomed for failure no matter how hard Cam "tried."

Taking a deep breath, I decided to let the words flow and forget my plan. I knew I needed to get this off my chest.

"Oh, and you might want to put a lock on your burner phone. Otherwise, your wife might find out that you're textin' a bunch of other bitches."

Unphased by my anger and completely ignoring the fact that I busted him for his secret phone, Cam moved from the bed, now standing several feet away from me, nearly on the opposite side of our hotel suite. With his arms crossed, looking as though he had better things to do with his time, Cam returned my emotional outpour with a cold, blank stare. For a second, I thought he was going to speak, but all he did was look at me, and he didn't look at me with adoring eyes, either. He looked at me like I was the enemy, as if he was disgusted with what he saw. The love in his eyes was gone, and I was met with a disdain and a look of death, as if to say, "And what, bitch?" Cam's ice-cold demeanor made the room feel unfamiliar and unwelcoming, and I wanted to run out as fast as I could, but I knew I had nowhere to go. I felt alone, and I realized I was arguing with a man I no longer knew. My safety net was in Atlanta, and I was thousands of miles away from home with no support system and no where to take a breather from this unexpected madness.

Throughout our relationship, Cam and I had hit our share of highs and lows, but he had never been indifferent toward me. Usually, he put on a show when he would try to get his point across, or he would beg me to stop crying. Sometimes, we would tear each other's clothes off, have sex, and pretend as if our fight never happened. Basically, he would always show some sort of emotion when we argued, even to the point of exaggeration. This time, however, he couldn't have cared less, and it was written all over his face and shown in his body language.

Suddenly, yet still silent, Cam removed a white envelope from his back pocket. He started to walk toward me, holding the envelope in his right hand. For a second, I wondered if he was about to console me. I also wondered what the hell was inside that envelope. Cam walked right past me and placed the envelope on top of the hotel desk.

"That's for you. Pack up your stuff and call a cab to take you to the airport. Your flight leaves in a couple of hours," Cam flatly said as he walked away and moved toward the door.

"My flight?" I said, feeling as if the wind was knocked out of my lungs. "What do you mean, Cam? You're sending me home?" I asked, panting as if I was struggling to find air. Yesterday, a flight home was exactly what I wanted, but this wasn't a ticket on my terms; Cam was kicking me out of L.A. and out of his life.

Cam ignored my questions and merely walked out of the hotel room without saying a word.

Feeling as if my entire world was crashing down, I

sprinted toward the door, opened it, and shouted down the hallway as Cam appeared to be walking toward the lobby.

"Cam!" I screamed. "Don't do this! Please, talk to me. Please!" I cried, still not giving a damn who heard. To think that he couldn't give me the decency of an explanation, let alone the respect of a response, shattered my heart into a million pieces. We may have been over, but to simply leave without a word left my heart in the bottom of my chest. He really left me alone in L.A., only to be sent home to an empty house and a broken marriage.

I ran back into the hotel room with tears in my eyes. My eyes continued to well with tears, and everything seemed blurry. I rushed over to my suitcase and carelessly started grabbing my clothes from around the room. Without folding my clothes or trying to arrange things with some sort of organization, I stuffed everything into my bag and zipped it shut.

"A cab," I mumbled to myself, yet again breaking down into tears of anger and confusion because Cam, my husband, wouldn't even so much as call his wife an Uber.

"Worthless motherfucker!" I screamed at the top of my lungs, almost wishing someone had heard so I could cry or vent to a willing participant.

This was the end, and there was nothing I could do about it, although at this point, I wasn't sure I wanted to ever give this man another chance as long as I lived. Wiping the tears from my eyes, I picked up my suitcase and proceeded to the lobby to call a cab. My time in L.A. was officially over, and this marriage was soon to follow.

.

CHAPTER SIXTEEN

Thanks to in-flight Wi-Fi, I was able to text the only person I could count on – my sister. Without really explaining what went down, I sent Brittany a text to let her know that Cam and I were finished and that I was on my way back to Atlanta.

Brit, it's over. Our marriage is done. I know you've heard it all before, but we're really done this time. There's no going back. I've spent the first part of my flight searching for a lawyer. Please, whatever you do, don't tell me that you knew this would happen. My heart can't take much more. I'll be back in Atlanta around dinner time. Can I come by your place when I land?

She replied within seconds, as I knew she would. I may have had an unreliable spouse, but I damn sure had a supportive, loving sibling.

Whatever you need me to do, I'm here. Send me your flight info so I can pick you up at the airport. We can talk then, k? Trust to relax, Jaz, please.

I sent Brittany my flight information, closed out my text messages, and stared at the seat in front of me in disbelief. As I adjusted my cramped legs, realizing there was no where for me to stretch or move, I couldn't help but think back to a week ago when Cam and I were happier than ever. Our first-class flight to L.A. ended in my solo flight in coach back to Atlanta. Tears started to roll down my cheeks, and I couldn't have cared less as to who noticed. I was sickened to my core, to think that I ever believed Cam could change and that I gave up a semester of school to fix a marriage I never broke in the first place. I began writing an email to the dean of my school, explaining that I had withdrawn for the semester but would like to immediately resume classes. I explained that I would do whatever it takes to catch up, timeline-wise, to my classmates, and make up for the time spent outside of the classroom. Up until this point, I had only missed four classes, so I hoped they would accept my plea to return to school rather than wait until the following semester.

I placed my phone in my purse, put my head back against the seat, and closed my eyes, knowing damn well I wouldn't fall asleep. I hoped to find some sort of peace during the long-ass flight to the East Coast, yet I knew the next four hours would feel like a lifetime.

**

As expected, Brittany was waiting for me at the airport when I touched down. I ran into her arms like a little girl who needed her mama.

"Brit," I wailed. "He sent me home without saying a word to me, just gave me a plane ticket and basically kicked me out," I cried.

"That piece of shit," Brittany seethed as she held me. "Before you change your mind about Cam, let's get your stuff from his place."

Agreeing with her plan, I loaded my suitcase into her car and drove toward Cam's apartment.

"I'll run into grocery store and see if they have any boxes we can take," Brittany said as she sped down the highway. "We can just throw everything inside some boxes and store them at my place."

Thankfully, Brittany drove an SUV, so I knew only one trip would be needed for this spur-of-the-moment move. A few minutes later, Brittany pulled into the grocery store parking lot, parked her car, and ran inside to see if they had a few boxes. As I waited in the car, I took out my phone and contemplated whether to scroll through Instagram and Twitter or wait until I calmed down a bit. I wasn't prepared to see or read anything out of pocket, so I figured I'd hold off. As I closed out both apps, my phone began to ring. It was Lew.

"Hello?" I answered, noticeably still upset yet not giving a damn if Lew or anyone else knew how devastated I felt.

"Jasmine, it's me," Cam said matter-of-factly.

"The fuck do you want, and why are you calling me from Lew's phone?" I asked, completely caught off guard by Cam on the other end.

"Because I'm changin' my number, and I don't want you to have it, that's why," he barked back.

I felt stunned, as if I couldn't register the words he was spewing into the phone.

"Why are you doing this to me?" I managed to ask as I started to bawl all over again. "I've never done anything to hurt you, and it feels like you're stabbing me in the chest, over and over again. What the hell did I do to deserve this, Cam?" I sobbed.

I couldn't believe how this relationship was spiraling out of control. First, he came back to our room a whole day later without trying to make an excuse or even speak. Then, he carelessly gives me a plane ticket home, a coach ticket at that. Now, he's telling me he's changing his number and doesn't want me to have it. This felt like hell, and I didn't deserve a gotdamn minute of it. I may have wanted a divorce, but I didn't want to be abused in the process. Our breakup was painful enough and accepting the fact that he had multiple affairs was torture, so to endure this treatment was the cherry on top of a shit sundae. The Cam I knew was dead and gone, and I was dealing with a full-blown narcissist.

Cam sighed heavily into the phone, and I could tell he felt some sort of emotion as I sobbed from the depths of my soul.

"Jaz, you're right. You don't deserve this shit, but I also don't think we should be married," Cam said, sounding a bit more human.

"We were fine before Mike came to L.A.! Cam, be real with me. What the fuck happened in the last couple of days that our marriage went to shit? Just tell me so this makes sense," I cried.

Cam paused, and I could tell he was contemplating whether to tell me the truth or just sugarcoat some lies. Either way, I knew I couldn't take his word, but I figured I'd listen to appease my sense of wonder.

"Man, I don't know. Shit, I was happy, but I look around and I don't think I can do this shit. I'm just bein' real with you, Jaz. Touring and the clubs, and the women. I don't know if I can do this shit, and I don't know if I want to, either."

I may have been crushed by his response, but I wasn't surprised by what he said, not at all. Cam was never strong enough to resist temptation, not forever at least, and that was clear as day after I found his secret phone in our suite that day.

In the back of my mind, I always knew it was only a matter of time until something like this happened.

"Alright," I sighed, strangely feeling a bit of relief after he told the truth for the first time in our marriage. "I'm grabbing some boxes now, and I'll be moved out of your place by the end of the day. Take care, Cam," I said, hanging up the phone. This was really it. We were done. He was done with his attempts in being a faithful husband, and I was done with my acceptance of his failures to be all he promised me he would be.

A few minutes later, Brittany returned with several boxes. She opened her trunk, placed them securely in the back, and slammed the door.

"Are you ready?" Brittany asked, referring to my emotional state, not exactly the move itself.

"I guess, whatever 'ready' means," I replied.

When we arrived at Cam's, I couldn't help but cry when we walked through the front door. I didn't get married to get divorced, yet that was exactly what happened. The generation curses I so badly wanted to change were repeating themselves before my very eyes, and my dream of having a secure, stable family was now nonexistent. Little by little, Brittany and I packed up my belongings, making sure not to leave anything behind. Brittany snagged a few of Cam's designer shoes, laughing about putting them on eBay.

"Shit, he wanna buy these hoes Chanel? Well, he can

buy himself some new shoes, too," she smirked.

Before leaving his apartment I turned on Cam's old iPad. I wanted to take one final glance at his message, not for any particular reason, but just to confirm the lowlife I knew he was.

"Jaz, what's the point? Brittany asked. "You've read everything you needed to read. You know he's a dog. Why do you want to torture yourself even more?"

"Girl, I don't know. Let me just close this chapter my way, please," I sighed, exhausted from the turn of events from the last 24 hours.

As I signed into Cam's iCloud, I saw more naked pictures and random texts to different girls about coming to his shows. Those came as no surprise. However, one text thread made me question whether I was seeing things or if what I read was really on the screen. It was a text from one of the women I happened to include in my group text from last night, the lesbian who was supposedly in love with her girlfriend. From the looks of this text, the other person she was in love with was my husband.

I love you, too, baby. I can't wait for you to feel the little kicks in my stomach. In six more months, we will meet our little prince or princess. Your timing was perfect. I'll see you later, Daddy.

I quickly reached to my side to grab the chair in front of me, as I thought I was going to pass out.

"Brittany, I need you to come here, please," I panted. I was too stunned to cry, and my world felt as if it suddenly stopped.

Brittany ran into the room, confused as to why I was in a daze.

"What is it, Jaz?" she confusedly asked.

I held out Cam's iPad, and nodded my head toward the device, motioning her to read the text that sent me into a downward spiral.

As Brittany read the message, I saw her eyes widen and her face harden.

After taking a deep sigh, Brittany turned to me, put her hand on my shoulder, and quietly said, "He's not your problem anymore, Jaz. Let him be her headache," she said as she tried her best to console me.

My husband got another girl pregnant, and this seemed to be anything but a surprise to him. The man who begged for me back, time and time again, had a whole mistress, and he apparently had a growing family, too. As my mind drifted off to a dark, dark place, my phone started to buzz, momentarily pulling me away from my thoughts. It was a text message.

Jasmine, click on this link. There's something you should see.

To be continued...